X6   7/16

P9-DGC-267

DISCARD

A Matter of Time

Printed in the United States of America
First Edition, April 2016
1 3 5 7 9 10 8 6 4 2

Library of Congress Control Number: 2015936654
FAC-008598-16057
ISBN 978-1-4847-2960-1

Book designed by Megan Youngquist Parent

disneybooks.com
disney.com/Alice

DISNEY
ALICE THROUGH THE LOOKING GLASS

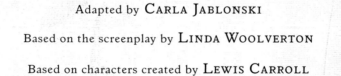

A MATTER OF TIME

Adapted by CARLA JABLONSKI

Based on the screenplay by LINDA WOOLVERTON

Based on characters created by LEWIS CARROLL

Produced by
JOE ROTH, SUZANNE TODD & JENNIFER TODD, TIM BURTON

Directed by JAMES BOBIN

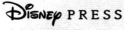

DISNEY PRESS
Los Angeles • New York

For those original adventure-choosers:
Edward Packer and R. A. Montgomery

And for Judy Gitenstein and Charles Kochman who
chose me to have adventures with the big boys.
—C. J.

To my mom and dad—thank you for always
encouraging my love of drawing.
—V. W.

For Mom, Dad, and Megan—your love and
support made me the artist I am today!
—J. T.

To my husband, Eddy, for his continued love and support.
—O. M.

To my mom, my brother, Larry, and Stephanie—
thank you for all your love and support.
—R. T.

THIS IS NO ORDINARY BOOK!

In this book *you* are the most important charac-ter, and *you* get to choose exactly who *you* are! Not only that, *you* also get to choose *when* you are! Yup! What you hold in your hands works just like the Chronosphere you will discover within these pages. That means this book is a kind of time machine—allowing you to move forward and backward.

BE CAREFUL, THOUGH:

what happens to you depends on what choices you make. So choose wisely. While you may not be able to change the past, you might just learn something from it. Your first choice is on the next page!

You stand in front of a mirror. "You don't have all day," you remind yourself. "Stop wasting time!"

There's just one last thing to do before you go.

You take a long look at your reflection.

If you:

Smooth your long blond hair and the brightly colored silk skirt of your gown, go to page 5.
You are Alice *now*.

Add one more of your father's hats to the two already on your head, turn to page 95.
You are the Hatter *then*.

Pick up an enormous powder puff and give your gigantic face a *poof*, go to page 159.
You are the Red Queen *now*.

Straighten your tiara, lift up your doll, and twirl, turn to page 197.
You are the White Queen *then*.

ALICE

YOU PEER out the carriage window as your mother fusses nervously beside you. She's worried about the two of you showing up to the Ascots' party uninvited.

"Don't worry, Mother," you reassure her. "I'll just run my business proposition by Hamish, and then we'll be out of there in a couple of shakes. Besides, as captain of the ship the *Wonder,* I need to give him my report."

"He may not be happy that you were at sea an extra year," your mother says as the carriage stops outside the Ascots' enormous mansion.

You think perhaps it's your *mother* who isn't happy about your lengthy voyage. You've been home only a few hours and already you've noticed how changed her circumstances seem.

The house is run-down, she has let the servants go, and she seems edgy and tired. *But,* you think with satisfaction, *once Hamish agrees to my plans, she will have nothing to worry about.*

The Ascot mansion is lit up with lanterns. The strains of lively music drift toward you. At the front door, a footman raises his eyebrows when he removes your cloak and catches sight of the traditional Chinese outfit you're wearing.

Noticing his reaction, your mother sighs. "I do wish you'd worn that yellow dress. . . ."

You run your fingers along the rich silk of the gown. "If it's good enough for the Dowager Empress of China, it's good enough for the Ascots."

Your mother shakes her head, frowning. "Please, Alice, must you be so headstrong?"

"Obviously I must," you quip, then dart toward the grand hallway.

The party is in full swing. As you scan the guests for familiar faces, Mr. Harcourt, Hamish's company clerk, approaches you with an anxious expression. "Miss Kingsleigh? What are you—"

"I've come to give my report to Lord Ascot," you explain. It feels odd to call Hamish that. The former Lord Ascot, Hamish's father, passed away while you were at sea. Unlike his son, he was a great man. You are truly going to miss him.

You break yourself out of your reverie as Mr. Harcourt leads you and your mother to a corner of the room where the hosts are greeting guests. Hamish looks smug—his usual expression—and his mother, Lady Ascot, is as imperious as ever. A young woman holding a baby stands beside Hamish. Seeing the infant's red hair, you surmise that he must be Hamish's son and the woman Hamish's wife.

When Lady Ascot notices you and your mother, she is momentarily flustered. You hope that your uninvited arrival doesn't cause a scene. You don't want to embarrass your mother. But Lady Ascot quickly regains her composure.

"Helen! What a surprise!" she tells your mother. Then she turns to you. "And is that Alice? My, the sea and salt air have done wonders for you. When you left you were so pale and peaked."

How's that for a backhanded compliment? "Thank you," you say politely.

You hate the way she's sizing up your mother in her less-than-perfect gown and how self-conscious this scrutiny makes your mother feel.

"Alice!" Hamish says. "Welcome home. Only a year late. We were afraid you might never come back with our ship!"

"*My* ship," you correct him quickly. Then, in an effort to keep things civil, you smile and add warmly, "Hello, Hamish."

The woman holding the baby sneers. "It is proper to refer to my husband as Lord Ascot. It is why we are having this little soiree, after all." She passes the baby to a nearby nanny, who drops a curtsy, then vanishes.

"Miss Kingsleigh," Hamish says, "this is my wife, Alexandra. The new Lady Ascot."

You've never been much interested in small talk, so you get down to business. "I've come to give my report, Lord Ascot."

"Ah, of course," Hamish says. "If you would follow me."

He leads you into a formal drawing room stuffy with cigar smoke. Six older men, not one under the age of sixty, stand around a large fireplace.

One of the men glances your way and raises an eyebrow. He nudges the man beside him, who looks over with disapproval. The rest glare at you with expressions of annoyance and outright disdain. You're not sure if *all* women would get such a frosty reception from this group of old fogies or if it's just you in particular.

"Gentlemen," Hamish announces, "allow me to introduce Miss Alice Kingsleigh. Miss Kingsleigh—the board."

Ah, so these gentlemen form the board of directors of the company. In other words, they're the ones who make all the decisions and pay all the bills—the people you need to win over.

"Gentlemen, we must move quickly!" you say with great enthusiasm. "The profits of my voyage—"

Hamish cuts you off. "Scarcely outweigh the costs."

You continue, "Further expeditions to Ta-Kiang or Wu-chang—"

But Hamish interrupts again. "There will be no further expeditions."

You gape at him. "What are you saying?"

Hamish shrugs. "The risks are not worth the reward."

"There are risks, indeed, but the possibilities are limitless!" you argue.

"An extra year at sea, Alice." Hamish shakes his head. "There were hard decisions to make in your absence."

This can't be happening. The voyages you've already planned! All *cancelled*? Just like that?

"But . . . what am I to do?" you ask, bewildered.

"There's a position in our clerking office," Hamish says. "You'll start in files. . . ."

The smirk on Hamish's face tells you all you need to know. "This isn't about China at all, is it?" you exclaim, fury rising. "It's because three years ago I turned you down when you asked me to marry you!"

You see a tiny flicker of doubt in his eyes, but he quickly straightens up and his expression hardens. "I'm sorry, Miss Kingsleigh. But that is all we can do for you. No other company is in the business of hiring female clerks, let alone as ships' captains!"

The six gentlemen board members let out loud guffaws and chuckles. This only makes you angrier. You are not going to let these ridiculous men push you around!

You hold your head up high. "I have voting rights and ten percent of the company," you declare, proud that you aren't letting your anger get the better of you. "Your father set those shares aside for me."

Hamish's slow smile seems almost triumphant. "Correction. He gave them to your mother, who sold them to me, last year, while you were gone. Along with the bond on the house."

This takes the wind out of your sails. "Her house?" you repeat.

"Secured by your father against the ship he bought."

Your chest grows tight. "The *Wonder*?" Your voice is barely a whisper. Beyond Hamish you can see Mr. Harcourt, the clerk. His is the only sympathetic face in the room.

"Yes, the vessel," Hamish confirms. "Sign it over and you'll redeem the house, receive a salary, and a pension."

"Give up the *Wonder*?" According to Hamish, your mother is in terrible financial straits. If you don't sign over your ownership of the ship, she will lose her home.

"It's the only way we can help you. And your mother." Hamish crosses to the large desk and locates a document. He holds out a pen and grins.

This is all too much.

Party guests complain as you race through the ballroom. You hear your mother call your name. You whirl around as she catches up to you.

"How could you sell our shares?" you demand.

"I had no choice, Alice," she says. "With your sister on her mission and you at sea for an extra year! What was I to do?"

You turn and march away. You'll suffocate if you stay in this dreadful mansion surrounded by all these people a moment longer. You find an open door and rush outside.

A bright moon illuminates the greenhouse. You enter, inhaling deeply, taking in the heady scent of the tropical plants. After all your travels, this exotic sanctuary feels more like home than the fussy rooms of the mansion. You lower yourself onto a bench and take out your father's broken pocket watch. It may no longer tell time, but you'd never part with it. It brings you such vivid memories of your father, a man you miss desperately. His belief in the impossible has always given you strength in times of trouble.

You stroke the stopped timepiece sadly. "Sign over the *Wonder* to become a clerk?" you murmur. "Just give up on the impossible?"

A movement catches your eye. A large blue butterfly perches on an orchid in front of you. It flutters, then holds still. You gaze at each other.

"Absolem?" you say uncertainly.

Could this actually be Absolem, once a caterpillar and

now a butterfly? Your friend from the time you visited the most fantastical, most wondrous world of all? Underland.

The butterfly flits away.

Should you follow it? If it is Absolem, he must have come here to find you!

But that's silly! He could very well be just an ordinary butterfly, not the wise caterpillar turned majestic butterfly you befriended in Underland. On the other hand . . .

IF YOU FOLLOW
THE BUTTERFLY, TURN TO PAGE 14.

IF YOU DON'T FOLLOW THE BUTTERFLY,
GO TO PAGE 13 AND
FLIP THE BOOK UPSIDE DOWN.

THAT CAN'T be Absolem, you tell yourself. You figure you're just upset and your mind is playing tricks on you.

"Alice?" Your mother hovers in the greenhouse doorway. In the moonlight you can see how frail she is, how worried. Things have not been easy for her in the years you have been gone. You know what you have to do.

You brush away a tear and force a smile. As much as you hate doing it, you feel it's the right thing. Your mother needs your help, and this is the only thing you can think of that will solve her problems.

You return to the party and find Mr. Harcourt. You don't think you could go through with this decision if you had to face Hamish's smug sneer. You tell Mr. Harcourt that you will agree to the conditions. You will sign the papers and become a clerk.

Sigh.

Continue on page 15.

YOU PURSUE the butterfly into the mansion's dining room. It dodges past guests, and you lose sight of it. Where could it be? You whip your head around frantically.

Then you spot it. It's perched on a chandelier above the dining table, as if waiting for you to catch up.

You hoist up the hem of your long skirt and climb onto the table. You pick your way among the punch bowls, platters of sweets, and fruit cornucopias.

"Alice! Get down from there!" your mother calls from behind you.

You feel multiple pairs of eyes on you, but you are determined to get to that butterfly. It's on the move again, heading toward the end of the table where Hamish is holding court.

The butterfly flutters near Hamish's head. He looks up and swats it onto the table. The butterfly teeters on the white tablecloth as if stunned.

"Bloody moths," Hamish mutters. He brings his hand down to squash the butterfly.

You leap onto Hamish, sending him flying to the ground.

Continue on page 17.

Being a clerk in Hamish's offices is just as awful as you had expected. You are miserable, buried under stacks and stacks of paper. One especially boring day, while listening to Hamish droning on about something dull, you absentmindedly start folding papers, just like the origami you saw in your travels. You make a little swan and keep it on your desk beside your lamp. Each day you add another creature to your paper menagerie. Soon you have quite a collection!

People love them. In fact, so many people ask where they can buy them that you decide to go into business.

You set up shop and become extremely wealthy creating all kinds of paper trinkets. The most popular turns out to be a tiny replica of your former ship, the *Wonder*.

You smile as you realize your ship brought you a fortune after all!

THE END

NOW THAT YOU'VE CRAFTED A LUCRATIVE
BUSINESS, GO BACK TO PAGE 2 TO TRY
YOUR LUCK AS SOMEONE ELSE!

You land on top of him and pummel him furiously. "How could you?" you shriek.

"Help!" Hamish cries. "Assault! Police! *Mother!*"

Chaos breaks out all around you. You don't care. "You brute!" you scream at Hamish.

"Get her off me!" Hamish whines. "Get her off!"

Lady Ascot's voice breaks through all the confusion. "Helen! Control your daughter!" she orders your mother imperiously.

Two sets of hands pull you off Hamish. The footmen back you up against the dining table. You have no idea what they have in mind for you, but you know it's not something you want to stick around for.

You reach behind you, feeling for something to use as a distraction. You grab two small finger bowls and fling them at the footmen's eyes. Instantly, one of them starts sneezing and tears stream down the other's face.

"Ah. Salt and pepper," you say. As a group of servants rush over, you spot the blue butterfly fluttering out of the room, toward the grand staircase. Once again, you give chase.

You vault up the stairs, taking them two at a time. Behind you, you hear people shouting.

"The girl's gone mad!"

"After her!"

"Don't let her get away!"

The blue butterfly turns a corner. You dash after it up

another flight of stairs and run along a dilapidated corridor. The footsteps keep coming. You have to hide. But where?

You try several doors, but they're all locked. Then a knob turns and you fling open the door. You duck into the room, pull the door shut, and lock it.

Your breath comes in gasps as you lean against the door. You gaze around your hiding place.

Dust-covered furniture fills the room. A burnished antique looking glass hangs above a marble fireplace with an ornate mantelpiece. On either side hang oil paintings. A chess set is laid out on a side table. The blue butterfly flits around you.

"Absolem? It *is* you, isn't it?"

The butterfly weaves and dips, and you follow it to the fireplace. You gaze up at the mirror and your mouth drops open.

The mirror is changing! The glass fogs, then swirls, turning into a bright silvery mist. You watch, transfixed, as the butterfly flies *into* the looking glass. A moment later, it's flying in the room you see reflected in the mirror.

You quickly check the room behind you. No butterfly. Your head whips back around. The butterfly continues its graceful arcs in the looking glass. The only explanation is that it really did fly *through* the mirror!

You take a step closer. "Curious," you murmur.

You reach out to touch the surface of the mirror. Your hand passes through it as if it were a pool of water. You yank your hand away. The sensation was so peculiar! You rub your hand, but it feels completely normal.

You hear heavy footsteps outside the door. The knob turns, but the lock holds. "Bring the key!" someone shouts.

You step onto the fireguard, then climb up onto the over-size mantelpiece. Kneeling, you touch the mirror again. Once more the surface shimmers as your hand breaks through. A key jangles in the door. You glance back at it, wondering what you should do.

WHY SHOULD YOU ALLOW THEM TO RUN YOU OFF? YOU CAN ALWAYS GO THROUGH THE MIRROR AFTER YOU'VE DEALT WITH THIS ANGRY MOB. GO TO PAGE 21 AND FLIP THE BOOK UPSIDE DOWN.

YOU'RE OUTTA HERE! GO TO PAGE 20 AND TRAVEL THROUGH THE LOOKING GLASS.

YOU PUSH your hand, then the rest of your body, through the looking glass. You emerge on the other side and gaze around in wonder.

"Curiouser and curiouser," you say.

You survey the room. It is the mirror image of the one you were just in. You turn to the mantel clock beside you. It now has an old man's face, which grins at you.

"Hello again, Alice!" it says.

The pictures on either side of the mirror come to life. "You shouldn't be here!" the stern woman in one oil painting says. "You're too old for this nonsense!"

"Oh, hush," says the serious-looking man in the other painting. "One is never too old!"

You leap down from the mantel onto a table. Chess pieces hop around and brush against a very fat egg-man perched on the edge.

"Not again!" he cries as he wobbles. "Uh . . . uh . . . ooooooh!"

He teeters, then falls to the floor and shatters. You wince,

Continue on page 22.

YOU'RE NOT going to let that mob scare you. You're going to stand up to them! The door is flung open, and you are roughly pulled down from the mantel by two footmen.

"He's the one you should be after!" you cry, pointing at Hamish as the footmen drag you toward the waiting policemen. "He is guilty of butterfly cruelty!"

You're taken to the loony bin. There you spend the rest of your life painting pictures of butterflies. Oh, well. It didn't turn out that great for you in . . .

THE END.

YIKES. ESCAPE THE MADHOUSE BY RETURNING
TO PAGE 2 AND STARTING OVER.

gazing down at the familiar fellow. If you recall correctly, that's Humpty Dumpty. And he just had another great fall.

From the floor, Humpty tries to make his unsmashed face look stoic. "Don't worry, dear!" he says. "I really ought to stop sitting on walls."

The white king from the chess set rallies. "All my horses, all my men," he orders, "to the rescue!"

The chess pieces jump into action. Pawns create lines down the table legs. The white knight slides down the fireplace poker leaning against the table. They reach the floor and attempt to piece Humpty together.

"Sorry! I'm so sorry!" you say, scrambling to the floor. You'd like to help but you have no idea how.

"Clumsy as ever," the blue butterfly says, landing on the carpet next to you. "I thought you'd never get the idea."

You'd recognize that superior tone anywhere.

"Oh, Absolem!" you exclaim. "It *is* you!" You'd hug him, but you fear that in his butterfly form he may be too delicate.

"You've been gone too long, Alice," he says. "Friends cannot be neglected."

That's a somewhat ominous greeting, you think. "Has something happened?"

"All will become clear in the fullness of time. For now, hurry. Follow that passage."

You'd forgotten how cryptic these Underland creatures can be. But you know Absolem well enough to do as he says.

You hurry to the door. As you turn the knob, Absolem adds, "Oh, and do mind your step." You glance back at him, puzzled, as you go through the door.

The next thing you know, you're falling! You scream as you plummet down, down, down through pink clouds.

You land in a floral arrangement—the centerpiece of a huge table. This must be your day for ruining dinner parties.

Staring at you from around the table are your old Underland friends: the chubby twins, Tweedledum and Tweedledee, clad in their usual matching striped outfits; the bloodhound, Bayard; McTwisp, the White Rabbit, looking dapper as ever in a dark blue coat and a pristine white shirt; the sleepy Dormouse, Mallymkun; and the wacky March Hare, Thackery Earwicket, raffish and rumpled.

It must be a very special occasion, because Mirana, the White Queen herself, sits at the head of the table, her white hair and white gown practically glowing in the sunlight. You notice the enormous Bandersnatch snoozing in the shade of one of the blossoming trees. You're in the White Queen's garden at Marmoreal Castle!

As you struggle to untangle yourself from the flower arrangement, you notice sketches of the Hatter covering the table. They're scribbled with notes such as "Best place to tickle," with an arrow leading to an X under his arm. Several drawings of the Hatter have areas circled and list "symptoms" to look out for. Puzzled, you look around at the group. They all wear serious expressions.

"Have I come at a bad time?" you ask.

"We were afraid you weren't coming at all," Mirana says.

"Whatever's the matter?" you ask.

"The Hatter's the matter," McTwisp replies, his white whiskers twitching.

"Or the matter of the Hatter?" one of the twins—Tweedledum?—says.

"The former," the other twin—Tweedledee?—responds.

"The latter!" Tweedledum insists.

"Tweedles!" Mirana scolds.

The Tweedles look chastened. Then, as one, they state very gravely, "He's mad."

Your forehead wrinkles in confusion. "Hatter? Yes, I know. That's what makes him so . . . *him*."

"But worse," Tweedledum says. "Denies himself laughter."

"Grows darker," Tweedledee adds. "Less dafter."

A toothy smile appears, floating above the table. Gradually, the rest of Chessur, the Cheshire Cat, appears. He gazes down at the sketches on the table.

"No scheme of ours can raise any sort of smile," he says. Although his grin is just as large as usual, he sounds sad. "We'd rather hoped you might help us save him."

"Save him? What happened?" you ask.

Somber glances are exchanged around the table. Finally, Mirana gives Bayard a tiny nod.

"We were playing our usual game of fetch," Bayard explains in his deep, rumbly voice. "I'd just tossed the stick and Hatter went chasing after it."

You smile as you picture the large bloodhound throwing the stick and Hatter bounding after it as if *he* were the dog.

"Hatter was perfectly Hatterish, until . . ." Bayard sighs.

"Until . . ." you press.

Bayard gathers himself and continues. "When Hatter snuffled around on the ground to pick up the stick in his mouth, he found something. Something that changed everything." He stops again, as if he can't bear to go on.

"What did he find?" you ask.

"Tell her," Thackery urges.

"A paper hat," Bayard says. "A teeny, tiny, itty-bitty blue hat."

"It may have been small," McTwisp says, "but its effect was huge."

"That was the start of it," Bayard says.

"Of what?" you ask. You still don't understand what the problem is, though it's clear something is seriously wrong.

"The grand decline," Mirana tells you.

"He's convinced his family are still alive," McTwisp says.

"Which has made him deadly serious," Bayard explains.

"Terminally sane," Tweedledum says sadly.

They are silent, contemplating this terrible fate. Tweedledee pulls out a handkerchief and blows his nose loudly. Then he does the same for his twin.

"We've tried everything," Bayard says. He lets out a mournful howl as the rest of the group cast down their eyes.

"And then we thought of you," Mirana says. She looks at you hopefully.

You nod slowly. They are counting on you. You won't let them down.

You push yourself up from the table. "Where is he?"

⁓⦕⦖⁓

The group accompanies you to Hatter's hat-shaped house.

"It's best you see him alone," Mirana says. "No telling what he'll do if he sees us."

You nod, then hurry up to the door. You're about to knock when it flies open.

Hatter stands in the doorway, staring at you. He barely resembles the Hatter you knew. His usually wild orange hair is now parted severely in the middle and combed down flat. He wears a neatly pressed dark gray suit. He looks *normal*. It's awful.

"Yes?" he says. He obviously doesn't recognize you.

"Hatter? It's me . . . Alice!" You reach out to hug him, but he shrinks away. Your arms drop to your sides.

"I'm not taking on any new heads now," he says. "Good day."

He slams the door.

Well, you can't just give up. You're going in whether he wants you to or not! You march into the hat-shaped house.

Hatter sits at a very organized desk, writing in a ledger. He looks up, surprised. "Miss, please. If you want a hat—"

"I don't want a hat. I've come to see *you*. I want to talk to you!"

"Well, if you don't want a hat, I'm quite certain I can't help you." He returns to scribbling in the ledger.

"But you *can* help," you insist, crossing to him and planting yourself beside his desk. "I just need you to be *you* again. Everyone does."

He slides his chair back a few inches away from you. "Don't bring any *funny* ideas here," he says, waggling a scolding finger at you. "This is a serious place."

The Hatter heads into a back room, muttering, "Highly serious man, my father. Very serious indeed."

You have to get through to him! You follow him into the back room.

A large family portrait hangs above the fireplace. In the center is a stern man in black. You look from the portrait to the Hatter. The man in the painting looks a lot like Hatter does right now. The hairstyle, the glasses, the suit. The serious expression. Dates beneath the portrait imply the people in it are deceased.

You nod toward the portrait. "Was that . . . ?"

Hatter gazes sadly up at the picture. "My family. Lost for many years. But now they're coming home!"

You frown. "But how do you know they're alive?"

The Hatter spins around and holds out a tiny blue paper hat. "I found this! Proof! A sign! A message! They're alive!"

"You yourself told me your family died," you say gently. "Long ago. . . ."

The Hatter paces, agitated. "I don't know who you are or what you're trying to do, but my family is not gallsackering dead!"

He points toward the door. "Get out!" he shouts. The effort of shouting almost topples him over. You move to help, but he waves you away.

Not wanting to upset him further, you leave. For a moment you stand staring at the door, stunned. You can't believe how changed he is. You turn and see your friends waiting, hopeful expressions on their faces.

You sigh. "He doesn't even know who I am. . . ."

Your friends' heads fall. You walk along the path, the others joining you in a sad procession back to Marmoreal Castle.

"It's as we feared," Mirana says. "He's caught a terrible case of the Forgettingfulness."

"The Forgettingfulness?" you repeat. This isn't any kind of illness you've ever heard of.

"It's when things go in one ear . . ." Tweedledum begins.

". . . and out the other two," Tweedledee finishes.

"It all goes back to the Horunvendush Day," Mirana explains.

"Horrible Horunvendush Day," the twins intone.

"It was supposed to be a lovely day at the fairgrounds," McTwisp says. "But then . . ." He shudders, making his whiskers tremble.

You frown. "But I don't understand why the Hatter—"

Mirana puts a hand on your arm, cutting you off. "Hatter has always blamed himself for his family's death," she explains. "We were all at the Horunvendush Fair. It was a lovely day. Until the Jabberwocky attacked." Her voice trembles with the memory. "The Hatter brought me to safety, but he never saw his family again. And he has lived ever since with the weight of their loss."

A sad smile hovers near your shoulder. "So you see, dear Alice," Chessur says, materializing completely, "like a tree, our present problem has its roots in the past."

You nod slowly. "I see." You bite your lip, frowning. "I think. . . ."

"Which is why we were hoping you might go back into the past," Mirana says, "and save the Hatter's family."

You stare at Mirana. "Go back in time? But how?"

"With the Chronosphere," Chessur says.

"I'm sorry, the Chrono-what?" you ask.

"The Chronosphere," Mirana says. "It's the heart that powers time. Legend has it, it lets one travel across the Ocean of Time."

"But why me?" you ask.

"None of us can use it, because we've already been in the

past," Mirana says. *"That* past, anyway. And if your past self sees your future self . . ." Her voice trails off.

"Yes? What happens if your past self sees your future self?" you ask.

"Well, no one actually knows," Mirana confesses. "But it's catastrophic."

You shake your head. "This sounds dangerous. And complicated."

"It's not impossible, merely *un*possible," Chessur says.

"Will you do it?" Mirana asks.

It's a completely crazy plan. You seriously doubt it can work—especially since you barely understand it! They're waiting for your decision.

IF YOU AGREE TO ATTEMPT
TO USE THE CHRONOSPHERE
TO GO BACK IN TIME, TURN TO PAGE 34.

IF YOU THINK THERE MUST BE A BETTER,
LESS RISKY WAY, TURN TO PAGE 33
AND TURN THE BOOK UPSIDE DOWN.

"The sun was shining on the sea, shining with all its
     might.
It did its very best to make the billows smooth and
     bright.
And this was odd, because it was the middle of the night."

No reaction. You drum your fingers on his table, trying to
think of something else that will get him to re-Hatter.

Word play! The Hatter loves a good pun. You lean forward, a mischievous twinkle in your eye. "I was speaking with
a fish the other day. He told me he was going on a journey, and
I asked, 'With what *porpoise*?'"

Hatter stares at you. "Don't you mean 'purpose'?"

Hmmm . . . This is going to take some more energy. You
start striding around the room, spewing out more and more
silly thoughts: "Once a mouse told me a very dry story. He had
a very a long *tail*, indeed.

"Did you know that the world spins on its *axes*? Hopefully, they're not terribly sharp.

"Have you ever seen a sailor's rope? Maybe *knot* . . ."

"Must you be so . . . mad?" the Hatter interrupts. "It's all
so silly. Time-wasting. Irritating, even."

You can't believe it. Other than annoying Hatter, your
antics have no effect . . .

Continue on page 35.

YOU SHAKE your head. "It is just too dangerous," you say. "Too much of a risk. For everyone. What if I change something that should never be changed? It could be a disaster!"

They put on brave faces, but you can see they're disappointed. "There must be another way to help Hatter," you insist.

You return to the hat-shaped house, formulating a plan. You'll jolly him into being himself again. In fact, you'll act exactly as you imagine the Hatter himself would. That should get him to remember what he's really like!

You enter singing one of his favorite songs. "Twinkle, twinkle, little bat," you belt out. "How I wonder what you're at."

"Do stop that," the Hatter says. "Singing is a very frivolous activity."

Oh, dear. You're going to have to try harder. The Hatter's favorite activities are *always* frivolous! He must be very sick indeed!

Rhymes! He always used to enjoy poetry. You recite:

"**H**ATTER IS Underland, and Underland is Hatter," you declare. "If he is in need, I will help him, no matter what."

"We rather hoped you might say that," Mirana tells you with a smile. The others clap and cheer.

"And where exactly is this Chronosphere?" you ask, eager to get under way now that you've made the decision.

"In the hands of Time, of course," Chessur says.

"Well, I suppose all things are," you say, amused by his philosophizing. "But where is it now?"

"In the hands of Time," Mirana repeats. "It's his."

You gape at Mirana. "I'm sorry. Time is a 'he'?"

"He lives in a void of infinitude," she explains. "In a Castle of Eternity. Which is where you will go to begin."

"To end the Hatter's de-Hatterization," McTwisp says solemnly.

❧

You stand in front of an enormous grandfather clock in a dusty, hidden room in Mirana's castle.

Continue on page 36.

. . . on *him*.

Unfortunately, *you* get stuck like this. You can't stop speaking in puns and cavorting about like a madwoman!

You decide to stay in Underland, where it won't seem strange at all.

THE END

ALL THESE FUNNY PUNS AND PUNNY FUNS ARE
GETTING TO BE TOO MUCH. THE QUESTION IS
TOO MUCH OF WHAT? IT MIGHT MAKE MORE
SENSE TO GO BACK TO PAGE 2, BUT DON'T
LET THAT PREVENT YOU FROM DOING SO.

You shiver, then recite the plan to yourself. "Get into the Castle of Eternity. Borrow the Chronosphere from Time, who is a 'who' and not a 'what.' Use it to travel back in time to Horunvendush Day. Save the Hatter's family from being killed and thereby save the Hatter. . . ."

That's all.

"Simple," Chessur says.

You see them all trade nervous smiles. You turn to enter the clock, resolved.

Mirana stops you with a light hand on your shoulder. "Time is extremely powerful and apparently quite full of himself. So mind your manners. He is not someone you want as your enemy."

You nod. "I understand," you say, even though you don't exactly. You turn and squeeze into the clock.

You find yourself at the edge of a seemingly infinite space. In the distance, across the black void, is a stark, imposing castle. There seems no way to get there.

It's eerily silent. All you can hear is the sound of your own breathing. Then—a distant ticking. You look down and your eyes widen.

Sweeping across the void is a colossal stone clock hand that extends from the distant castle. It sweeps toward you with an unerring *tick*. Then you understand. You are inside an enormous clock—perhaps the clock that runs the entire Universe. Judging from its relatively swift movement, you're looking down at the clock's second hand.

You wait for the second hand to sweep your way, then take a deep breath and jump. You land safely and let out a long exhale of relief. Balancing carefully, you walk across the giant moving hand toward the castle.

You take another deep breath for courage and push open the massive door.

You enter a vast chamber, and the only sounds you hear come from the movement of gigantic cogs and gears. You stride along walkways high above a cavernous space filled with clockworks.

You come to a doorway and peek inside. A large man sits sleeping on a gigantic throne. *Man* isn't exactly the right word, though. He's part clockwork, and a small vent emits steam from his head as he breathes. His bushy mustache flutters with each exhale.

Is this Time? you wonder. *Does Time sleep? Is that why sometimes Time seems to pass so slowly? And when will Time be finished with his nap?* As if reading your thoughts, he startles awake, making you jump back.

What did Mirana tell you about him? Oh, yes. You should mind your manners.

"Good day, sir," you say politely from the bottom step leading up to the throne. "I'm sorry to bother you, but I was wondering if you might have time to speak with me?"

"Time? I have all the time in the world, young lady," he says "The question is . . . will I spare any for you?"

"That *is* the question, sir."

"Do you promise to be amusing?" he asks, tapping his gloved fingers together.

That's an odd request. Though from your previous dealings in Underland, you're pretty used to being asked strange things. "I don't know if I can promise that," you admit. "It's rather a serious subject."

"Well, I'm a rather serious person, myself," he replies. "For I am Time. The infinite. The immort—wait, what time is it?" He opens his cloak. His chest is an ornate timepiece!

"Hang it all! How infinitely ironic! I'm going to be late! Me!" He strides out of the room, his long cloak flapping behind him. "How could time get away from *me*?"

You dash after him. Endless hallways stretch out in many directions. "Wait!" you call. If you lose track of Time, you'll be lost forever in this crazy maze of a castle.

You hurry alongside him. He nods toward your pocket. "Why do you carry that fallen soldier?" he asks.

How did he know? You pull out your father's broken pocket watch.

Time eyes the watch. "A fine-looking instrument. Though I'm afraid its time has expired."

"My father was a great man," you tell Time. "His watch reminds me that nothing is impossible. I wouldn't part with it for anything in the world."

"Everyone parts with everything eventually, my dear," Time says.

You enter another cavernous chamber. An incredibly

elaborate timepiece stands in the center, its metronomic *tick-tock* booming through the room.

Time waves a sweeping arm toward it. "Behold!" he announces. "The Grand Clock of All Time!"

You see a spinning, glowing metallic sphere deep within the Grand Clock. It can only be the Chronosphere!

But Time starts walking again, so you follow. He leads you into a comfortable oak-paneled sitting room. He sits in a large overstuffed chair beside the roaring fireplace.

"Now. Ask your question," Time instructs you. "You have one minute exactly."

"It's about the Hatter, Tarrant Hightopp," you explain. "You see, the Jabberwocky killed . . ."

Time looks bored, opens his chest clock, and moves the second hand forward.

Suddenly, you're speaking so quickly you're amazed your mouth can keep up! He must have sped up time! ". . . his familyontheHorunvendushDayandI'dlikeyour permissionifyou pleasetoborrowtheChronosphere!" You pause, catching your breath and hoping he understood your rapid-fire delivery.

Time's eyes narrow. "How do you know about the Chronosphere?"

"I-I'd like to borrow it," you say.

"Borrow it? *Borrow it!* The Chronosphere powers Time oneself! It is not something to be 'borrowed' like a croquet mallet or a pair of hedge clippers!"

"But—"

"You are asking me to violate the logic of the Universe." Time stands up and walks to the door. He opens it for you. "The answer is no."

"But—"

"You are not amusing. Wilkins!" he shouts out the door. "Escort this trespasser out!"

Is your mission going to end here? Now?

Should you try to amuse him? That seems to be what he wants. Or should you leave quietly and try to come up with another plan?

IF YOU TRY TO AMUSE HIM,
GO TO PAGE 41 AND FLIP THE BOOK.

OR YOU CAN LEAVE THE ROOM
AS HE ASKED AND GO TO PAGE 44.

YOU HOPE that if you amuse Time he'll be more open to helping you. But what could possibly be amusing to a being like Time?

"Um, let's see . . . er . . . I know!" Your face lights up as a few jokes you think he might like pop into your head. "If five dodos run after one gryphon, what time is it?"

Time strokes his mustache, pondering the question.

"Five after one!" you declare.

His eyes widen a moment, and then he lets out a guffaw.

Phew! This could work. "So about the Chronosphere . . . ?" you ask.

He gestures for you to continue. "Tell another!"

"All right . . . um . . . a very silly chess pawn asked a rook what time it was, and the rook answered four forty-five. 'Why do you look so confused?' the rook asked. 'It's the oddest thing,' the pawn replied. 'I've been asking that question all day, and each time I get a different answer!'"

Time slaps his leg hard, chortling. "More, more!"

"Knock-knock," you say.

"Pardon?" Time asks.

Continue on page 43.

WHILE TIME MAY THINK YOU A HOOT, YOUR
FRIENDS MIGHT NOT FIND IT SO AMUSING
TO BE FROZEN IN TIME. TO GET HIM MOVING
AGAIN, GO BACK TO PAGE 2 AND TRY AGAIN.

"It's a knock-knock joke," you explain. "You have to ask 'who's there?'"

"Ah. Who's there?" He looks intrigued.

"It's Time."

He straightens up, excited. "It's Time who?"

"It's Time for another joke!"

Time claps. "Delightful! Delightful!"

"Will you remember me in a month?" you ask.

"You?" Time smiles at you warmly. "The most amusing person I have met in some time? Yes, indeed!"

"Will you remember me in a week?"

"Certainly!"

"Knock-knock," you say, suppressing a grin. You have a feeling he's going to like this one.

"Who's there?" he asks, a little confused by the abrupt change in the conversation.

"See? You forgot me already!"

"You are definitely amusing, my good lady!" He laughs. And laughs. And laughs.

The problem is, you are so entertaining Time forgets himself. Time stands still—forever!

THE END

of everything

Y OU SEE that you'll never be able to change his mind. You bow politely. "Sorry to bother you," you say, then turn to go.

"Young lady . . ." Time begins.

You turn back to face him. He's gazing at you with a penetrating stare. "You cannot change the past. It always was. It always will be. Although I daresay, you might learn something from it."

"Thank you for your time, sir," you say. You follow his assistant, Wilkins, into the corridor.

Suddenly, a shrill female voice calls from the entrance hall. "Oh, tick-tock!"

At the sound of the voice, Wilkins stops in his tracks. You stop, too.

"Miss, would you mind seeing yourself out?" he asks, looking pale. Without even waiting for your response, he hurries off. You frown. What was *that* about?

You hear echoing footsteps heading your way. You quickly hide behind one of the floor-to-ceiling tapestries lining the hall.

Time strides down the hallway, then stops in front of

a mirror. He considers his appearance, trying out various smiles. Then he cups a hand and breathes into it, checking his breath.

He's getting ready for a date! you realize. You fight back a laugh.

A bell rings through the castle. Time looks up, annoyed. "Ugh . . . will these interruptions never end?" he complains. He marches off.

You secretly follow him until he stops in front of a room with a sign: UNDERLANDIANS: LIVING. He enters, leaving the door wide open. You peek inside. Thousands of open-faced pocket watches hang from chains, ticking in limitless blackness.

"Who has stopped?" he asks as he passes down the endless line of watches. "Who has ticked their last tock? Tocked their last tick?"

He holds up his hand. A chain drops down, delivering a stopped watch to his palm. He looks at the name on the casing. "Ah, Brilliam Hinkle. Time's up."

He snaps the watch closed and exits on the other

side of the room. You scurry after him. Now he enters a room marked UNDERLANDIANS: DECEASED. This room is silent, filled with closed pocket watches. You observe as he flicks through a row of watches, reading the names engraved on their backs.

"'Higgens, Highbottom . . .'" he mutters. He pauses at a gap, then shrugs and moves on. "'Highview, Himmelby' . . . ah, 'Hinkle.'"

Time gently hangs the watch on an empty chain. "I hope you used your time well. Good night."

This must be what happens when anyone in Underland dies, you realize.

You're startled by footsteps behind you in the hallway.

A dark shadow on the floor gets larger and larger as the person approaches. A shadow with an enormous head. It's the Red Queen, Iracebeth!

You've got to get out of here!

You quickly retrace your steps to the empty Chamber of the Grand Clock. You hesitate a moment; then, reminding yourself what's at stake, you squeeze into the clock.

You are crammed tightly among millions of interlocking pieces moving together in the world's most intricate timepiece. And deep within, at its center, just visible past the swinging pendulums and spinning gears, glows a silver light.

"The Chronosphere . . ." you murmur. You reach out and grab it.

It crackles wildly in your hands. Scared but determined, you yank it hard to detach it from the gazillion widgets, gewgaws, and thingamajigs holding it in place. You hear an enormous cracking sound, like a thousand lightning strikes.

You leap out of the clock—and discover Time waiting for you.

Uh-oh.

Armies of ticking men swarm into the room. "Stop her!" Time bellows. "Seconds into Minutes!" he orders. "Minutes into Hours!"

The ticking men gather together, forming larger and larger units. A towering mechanical man lurches toward you. "My Hour," Time hollers, "get that Chronosphere!"

You stumble backward and trip, dropping the Chronosphere. Its lights start to pulse. With a blinding flash it expands into enormous revolving brass rings.

Without a second thought you run inside the Chronosphere's spinning rings. You face an impossible array of levers, switches, chains, and buttons. One lever has a note dangling from it: PULL ME.

So you do.

The Chronosphere instantly rolls forward, gathering momentum. You fly out the door of the Chamber of the Grand Clock.

The bands on the Chronosphere revolve faster and faster, the whirring sound increasing in pitch and volume as the vibrations jar your bones. Then, suddenly, *POOF!*

The world around you melts away and you find yourself above a vast ocean: the Ocean of Time.

The days are transparent beneath you. You see Time's castle directly below and all around you a patchwork quilt of all the days in history. You begin to move into the past.

Soon you spot flames on the horizon. Then you hear the terrifying screech of the Jabberwocky!

"Horunvendush Day!" you exclaim.

That is your destination. You must get to that day and save the Hatter's family.

You pull a combination of levers, and the Chronosphere spins down into the ocean—straight into Horunvendush Day.

<hr />

"Wh-what happened?" you murmur. You're lying on the ground, the Chronosphere beside you. It's back to its normal size. "Need to work on landing," you mutter. You roll over, grab it, then sit up and glance around.

The field is a charred, smoking ruin. You stand slowly, horrified by the devastation around you. A silent young man gazes down at a burning top hat. The Hatter! He seems lost, broken even.

"Hatter?" you call gently.

But this younger version of the Hatter just runs off. You are about to call out again when you hear thundering hoofs. The Red Queen's knight, Stayne, rides toward you, Vorpal sword in hand. You dive for cover and peer out from behind some bushes to watch him.

He carries a small burlap sack—which appears to be moving. You wonder what he captured, since it seems as though he has living creatures in that sack. You feel bad for whatever—or whomever—his prisoners may be.

Stayne's horse rears and whinnies as he pulls it to a stop beside Iracebeth. She's also on horseback, gazing down on the wrecked fairgrounds. She smirks, and then she and Stayne ride off.

They're up to something; you're sure of it. But you must stay focused on your mission—to help the Hatter!

You sadly look around at the scorched fairgrounds. Everything is still smoking. You are too late!

You trudge through the destruction. As you pass an old oak tree stump, a bright color catches your eye. You stop to see what it is.

You peer into the hollowed-out stump. "The blue hat!" you exclaim. What does it mean? You reach for it, but a strange screeching startles you. It sounds as if some ancient door is being wrenched open.

Your jaw drops as you see a rip opening in the sky. A bizarre contraption, kind of like a railroad handcar, tears through it. Steering it is Time himself. It seems he has built a clunky, hand-powered time machine.

"Give me what is mine!" Time demands. "You have no idea of that in which you dabble!"

You throw the Chronosphere to the ground. It immediately opens into the glowing sphere. You jump in and it begins to move. It rises from the ground, and Horunvendush Day melts away into the Ocean of Time.

You glance over your shoulder. Time is still on your tail, powering his handcart and getting closer.

He catches up with you. "You cannot win a race against Time!" he huffs. He's out of breath from his efforts. "Give it back. I am merciful. But you must give it back!"

He lunges for you.

You need to get somewhere—or, rather, some*when* fast!

DO YOU GO FORWARD IN TIME?

GO TO PAGE 51 AND FLIP THE BOOK.

DO YOU GO BACKWARD?

GO TO PAGE 52.

OOPS! YOU went *way* too far into the future! Nothing is familiar, everything is strange, and there are bizarre flying contraptions zipping around overhead. The plants and animals are odd shapes and colors—even odder than usual for Underland.

You're still the same age, but everyone else is the great-great-great-grandchild of the people you knew. There are identical twin girls wearing matching polka-dot shirts who can only be descendants of the Tweedles. There's also a partially visible Chessur-like tabby lounging in a tree. You even come across a grumpy caterpillar—a dead ringer for Absolem.

The problem is, the Chronosphere has aged. It's all rusty and cracked and no longer glows, not even a little. It just wore out.

This means you're stuck where you are.

Oh, well. You've always been ahead of your *time*!

THE END

Continue on page 53.

YOU YANK the lever hard, hoping you're going back to a day that will help you with your mission to restore the Hatter to himself again. You spin out of control and crash-land.

You dust yourself off and look around. There's no sign of Time, which is a good thing. But you have no idea where you are. Or when.

You hear trumpets blowing a fanfare. You head toward the noise.

You join a procession of Underland citizens approaching a castle. Humans, animals, and fanciful creatures have come from far and wide for some kind of celebration, you surmise. You follow them inside.

You stand at the back of the enormous formal room. A king and queen sit on thrones on a stage. On either side of them are two young women. Your eyes widen when you realize who they are: Mirana and Iracebeth—the White Queen and the Red Queen! Only they're in their twenties and must still be princesses.

Continue on page 54.

SPENDING TIME WITH THE DESCENDANTS OF
YOUR LOVED ONES IS DELIGHTFUL, BUT YOU
MISS YOUR OWN FRABJOUS FRIENDS. FLIP
BACK TO PAGE 2 AND START A NEW TALE.

Mirana is a beauty all in white. Her sister, Iracebeth, scowls next to her, dressed in red. Although her head is oversize and she's wearing her hair in that odd heart-shaped style, it's not as large as it was—is?—the last—*next*—time you saw her.

This time travel is wreaking havoc with your tenses!

A serious-looking man places a tiara on Mirana's head. When he steps back you recognize him as the man in the portrait in the Hatter's house. This must be Zanik Hightopp, the Hatter's father.

And there's the Hatter! He's younger than the day the Jabberwocky struck, so you've gone farther back in time. He opens a very large hatbox and holds it up to his father. Zanik takes out an enormous tiara. He stands behind Iracebeth, struggling to get the sparkling tiara on her very large head. Hatter stifles a laugh.

Finally, Zanik shoves the tiara down onto her head. It breaks in two.

The whole crowd bursts out laughing. Iracebeth turns purple with rage. She raises a finger to the sky and yells, "OFF WITH THEIR HEADS!"

The crowd goes silent. You almost feel bad for her, especially when her father announces that because of her behavior she is no longer the heir to the crown—*Mirana* is.

That sends Iracebeth over the edge. You and the crowd gasp as her head swells in front of your eyes.

Iracebeth marches over to the Hatter's father. "Zanik Hightopp," she hisses into his face, "I will never forget what you and your family have done to me this day. Never!"

Iracebeth storms off, followed by a tearful Mirana. The king and queen bid the crowd good day, and the citizens disperse.

Zanik watches them go, then turns on the Hatter, furious. "You cost the princess her crown!" Zanik says. "Do you know what this means for us?"

Zanik Hightopp and the Hatter squabble, speaking over each other. Then they both stop abruptly and stare at each other in silence.

You can see that Hatter is deeply pained by what his father has said to him. He storms past you and out into Witzend Street.

You jog to catch up. "Excuse me?" you call after him. "Tarrant!"

The Hatter whirls around, ready to argue. You rush up to him and fling your arms around him. "It's you, isn't it? It's really you!"

He looks down at you, confused. "I'm sorry. Have we met?"

You release him and grin. "Yes! I mean no! I mean, not yet. I'm Alice."

He cocks his head and studies you. "Funny. I feel I should know you."

"We met once, when I was young," you explain.

"I'm afraid I don't recall," the Hatter says.

"Because it hasn't happened yet," you say.

"When will it happen?" the Hatter asks.

"Years from now," you reply. "When you're older."

"I'll meet you when *you're* younger—and *I'm* older?" he says, puzzled.

"It doesn't make much sense, I know," you admit.

"Of course it does. You're Alice, my new, old friend." The Hatter gives you an amused smile as you walk together. "You're bonkers, aren't you?"

"Am I?" you ask.

"All the best ones are."

The Hatter stops beside a grand oak tree with a hole in its side. He grabs your arm. "Can you keep a secret?" he asks, his voice dropping to a whisper.

You step in closer to him.

"This tree is magical," he says, admiring it. "Every night when I was a boy, I would make a wish and the next morning the tree would have granted it. Usually green-and-white Swizzles. Delicious!"

He pats the tree, then walks on. You suddenly remember your mission.

"Wait! Stop! Your family is in danger!" you cry. "You must warn them about Horunvendush Day!"

"You want me to get a message to my family?" The Hatter narrows his eyes suspiciously, then points an accusing finger at you. "If my father sent you to change my mind, you can tell him that I never will!" He stomps away.

"Tarrant, wait! Listen!" you call out to him. "You are right now creating a past you will never be able to change. Hatter!"

But he's gone. Maybe you can warn his father instead.

◦⁓◦

"My sister wasn't always like this. But something happened when we were small," you hear Princess Mirana saying to the Hightopps as you approach the castle. "One snowy night—a night known forever as Fell Day—she was running through the town square and hit her head on a grandfather clock. Right at the stroke of six." She covers her eyes and shudders. "It changed everything."

This gives you an idea! You'll prevent the Red Queen's accident when she was a child. That way she won't grow up to be such a meanie! The Hatter and his father won't get into their argument, which means they'll be together on Horunvendush Day. Perhaps they'll *all* survive the Jabberwocky attack! And the Hatter *then* will become the Hatter *now*.

Well, not so much now, you think as you throw the Chronosphere to the ground. It pops open and you climb in. *The* now *before he lost his muchness.*

You shake your head. You'd better solve this problem soon, or you'll be as mad as, well, as the Hatter *should* be!

"Hang on, Hatter," you cry, as you zoom farther into the past.

You soon land on the outskirts of Witzend. A light snow is falling, so you know you must be pretty close to Fell Day.

A tiny set of grinning teeth floats around the corner, followed a few inches behind by a tiny kitten butt and tail.

You giggle. That must be Chessur as a kitten, before he got his materializing under control. A bloodhound puppy who can only be Bayard gives chase. A pair of chubby twins you immediately recognize as the Tweedles clumsily trot into view, followed by an eight-year-old Hatter.

"Tarrant!" a stern voice calls.

You and little Hatter both turn to see a younger Zanik Hightopp glaring at him from the doorway of his shop. Little Hatter sighs and trudges toward his father's shop. When he spots you, his face lights up. He grabs your hand and drags you into the shop.

The shop is neat and well organized. Hats sit atop stands on a counter. Trimmings are displayed along one wall, and stacked rolls of fabric wait to be selected. Zanik is writing in a large ledger.

"Papa! Look!" the little Hatter announces. "A customer with a lovely head."

"I'm sorry, miss," Zanik says. "We're closed." He stands and crosses the room.

Little Hatter tugs on Zanik's coat as he walks to the door.

"Papa, look! I made something for you in school!" He holds up a little blue paper hat.

Your eyes widen. The blue hat! The Hatter's downward spiral started when he found it. Here it is now! What does this mean?

You watch as the Hatter's father accidentally rips the hat. He shrugs and tosses it into the trash. Little Hatter runs upstairs, tears in his eyes. Poor little fellow!

Zanik looks thoughtful for a moment, then opens a drawer in his desk. You notice with surprise that it is full of green-and-white Swizzles. Hmmm . . . You leave the shop, feeling bad for the little Hatter.

You gaze up at the clock tower: 5:55 p.m. Five minutes before the fateful event that Mirana says changed her sister. The snow is swirling more forcefully. You need to get to the town square!

You hurry into the snowy cobblestone square just as the bell in the clock tower lets out a loud *gong!*

"The stroke of six!" you exclaim. "That's when it's going to happen!"

You look around for Iracebeth. A gentleman fish slides by upright, holding an umbrella. Two frog deliverymen struggle with the grandfather clock they carry.

Another booming *gong!* Then you see her: little Iracebeth running toward the square. Tears stream down her face, and she's not paying attention to where she's going.

She's heading straight for the frog deliverymen! And they don't see her! That must be the clock she hits her head on!

GONG!

Hurry! The bell has rung three times already—only three more gongs to go!

You have to stop this accident. But how?

THROW YOURSELF IN FRONT OF HER,
GO TO PAGE 61, AND FLIP THE BOOK.

OR STOP THE DELIVERY FROGS FROM
COLLIDING WITH HER AND TURN TO PAGE 62.

YOU FLING yourself at Iracebeth. But you slip on the ice and smash your *own* head into a large statue of King Oleron at the edge of the square.

Owwwwwww!

You gingerly feel your head to see if you're bleeding. *Phew.* You're not. That's a relief. But you're a little worried when you feel how much your head is swelling. This is more than a goose egg. It's already beginning to feel like a Jabberwocky egg.

Uh-oh.

Iracebeth tries to help you up, but your enormous head throws off your balance. The two of you topple over. Iracebeth hits her head, too. It instantly puffs up.

But things work out okay. You become her special friend, and she becomes a

Continue on page 63.

YOU DIVE for the front delivery frog and shove him—hard. The grandfather clock hits the ground with a chiming crash.

"Hey! What the—" the frog sputters.

Gong! The fourth gong! Hooray! You averted disaster!

Then you gasp. Little Iracebeth avoids the delivery frogs, thanks to you, but she's about to run into the gentleman fish!

"No! No! No!" you shout.

"Careful, miss!" the gentleman fish scolds.

Gong!

Just in time, Little Iracebeth veers out of the gentleman fish's path. But she skids on the ice. She slips, she slides, she windmills her arms, trying to keep her balance.

You can't watch! You cover your eyes just as the final gong sounds.

Wham! You peek through your fingers to see little Iracebeth hit her head on the base of a statue of her father, King Oleron. You wince.

"Just at the stroke of six," you say sadly. Exactly as Mirana had said.

Continue on page 64.

very sweet princess who grows up to be a very nice queen—all because she's not lonely anymore. There's another Big Head in town. *You!*

⌒⌒⌒

THE END

HAVING SUCH A GLORIOUSLY BIG HEAD IS
GETTING SOMEWHAT HEAVY. TURN BACK TO
PAGE 2 AND TRY ON ANOTHER HEAD FOR SIZE.

Iracebeth sits up, clutching her head. "My head!" she wails as people start to gather and try to help her up.

You sigh. "Time was right. You cannot change the past. She hit her head anyway."

You turn away sadly, unsure of what to do next. Movement in the Hatter's shop across the street catches your eye.

You peek through the window of the hat shop and watch Zanik Hightopp bend down and take the crumpled blue paper hat from the trash. He smooths it out, smiles to himself, and places it in his breast pocket. He gives the pocket a fond pat.

"He kept it," you murmur. This is important, somehow. Your brain reels as you try to put all the pieces of the puzzle together. The blue hat the Hatter just found, in *your* time. It's the very same hat his father kept from *this* time. And the same hat you discovered hidden in the tree stump on that fateful day of the Jabberwocky attack.

And where have you seen those green-and-white Swizzles before? In the Hatter's "magical" tree *and* in his father's desk drawer!

Something else . . . something else. The answer flashes into your head. When you were spying on Time in his castle, he went through the watches of the Underland citizens who had died. The closed watches were in alphabetical order.

"There was a gap!" you cry.

A gap where the Hightopps would have been. *If* they were no longer living.

"They're alive! They're *alive*!" You have to tell the Hatter!

You're finally getting the hang of traveling by Chronosphere. Soon you are back to the right time and place. You burst into the Hatter's house.

"Hatter! Your family! They're alive!" You look around. No sign of Hatter. *Hmmm*. Maybe you're *not* in the right time and place.

You go upstairs to check. Your heart clutches when you see Mirana, the Tweedles, Bayard, McTwisp, and Mallymkun crowded around the Hatter's bed. He lies dreadfully still with eyes closed. His once bright orange hair is now completely white.

McTwisp is listening to Hatter's chest with a stethoscope. He shakes his head. The others wear grave expressions as they acknowledge your arrival.

"The Forgettingfulness . . ." Tweedledee begins sadly.

"It's unfilled his head," Tweedledum finishes, equally sadly.

"We fear you are too late." Mirana sighs.

You take the Hatter's hand. "You were right," you tell him. "They're alive!"

No response.

"I can't bear to see him like this. . . ." Mallymkun chokes out.

Bayard picks Mally up in his mouth, and the group sadly departs, leaving you and the Hatter alone. You see the little blue paper hat on the nightstand. You pick it up.

You perch on the edge of his bed. "I know what this means, Hatter!" you say. You gently close his hand around the little hat. "You made it for your father."

Still no response. You fight back tears and continue. "And remember the magic tree, Hatter? It wasn't magic . . . it was *him*." You pat his hand. "All those years it was your father leaving those Swizzles for you to find. And on the day the Jabberwocky attacked he left the blue hat there as a message. That they'd survived!"

Did his eyelids twitch? Encouraged, you press on. "Because he kept it, Hatter. That blue hat you thought he threw away. All his life, a token of his love—his love for you, his son."

Definite eye flutters! You're getting through to him!

"And he *still* loves you, Hatter. Because he's still alive!"

The Hatter opens his eyes slowly. "He . . . kept it?" he asks groggily.

"Yes!" you exclaim. "I was there! I saw him pick it up out of the trash! Your family is alive!"

The Hatter struggles to sit up. He looks at you as if waking from a dream. He studies you carefully. "I'd know you anywhere. You're Alice!"

You smile. He's back! He's really and truly back to being himself!

"Oh, Hatter, I've missed you so much!" You want to laugh and cry and shout all at the same time. You hug him tightly.

Color comes back to his face, and his white hair slowly

turns orange again. When you pull away he looks down at the paper hat in his hand. "But why have they not come home?"

You figured out the answer to this one on the trip back to the present. You know what Stayne was doing with the Red Queen when the Jabberwocky attacked. What was wriggling in that sack. Whom Iracebeth had threatened all those years before.

"Because they are being held captive," you say. "By the only person cruel enough to keep them locked up all these years—"

"The bloody Big Head," the Hatter growls.

He leaps up and stands on his bed, aflame with purpose. "I'm going to find the Red Queen. And bring my family home!"

Very soon you and your friends have arrived at the top of a large hill. You and the Hatter balance on the Bandersnatch. Bayard carries Mally. Thackery and the Tweedles ride in a horse-drawn cart. Mirana is in the saddle of her white horse, with McTwisp holding on for dear life behind her.

You gaze down at the gigantic red heart-shaped castle, Iracebeth's stronghold in the Outlands.

"My family is there!" Hatter declares. "I know it."

"And if they are, we'll rescue them," you promise.

You and the gang enter a vast hall made of plants and

dirt. Roots rise from the mud floor, forming a grand staircase at the far end. Corridors lead off in all directions. The castle rustles and creaks, a creepy living entity.

How will you ever find the Hightopps in this maze of a palace?

"Is this where we . . . ?" McTwisp trails off, his nose twitching nervously.

"Split up!" Mallymkun brandishes her tiny sword.

You wonder who you should go with. You're reluctant to part from the Hatter, especially since this is a mission to save his family. But then you see the Tweedles absentmindedly pulling at the various vines on the wall. They'd probably be more focused if you went with them.

IF YOU GO WITH THE HATTER,
TURN TO PAGE 72.

IF YOU GO WITH THE TWEEDLES,
FLIP THE BOOK AND GO TO PAGE 69.

YOU AND the twins creep along the bizarre, vegetation-covered corridor. You know you're in the Red Queen's castle, but it's as if you're tramping through a jungle! You have to keep quieting the Tweedles. They have a comment and counter-comment about *everything*!

"We're being sneaky," you remind them, "so hush!"

"Hush and rush," Tweedledum tells his brother, grabbing his arm so that they move faster.

"Contrariwise, hush and *shush*!" Tweedledee protests.

"Please!" you whisper hoarsely. "We don't want anyone to know we're here!"

You continue along the mossy hall, the vines and leaves shuddering and slithering around you. You hear a steady *drip, drip, drip* as the humidity makes the castle a sopping steam room.

Tweedledum flicks open an umbrella. Tweedledee quickly joins him under it.

Where did he find that? you wonder. "Do you think it's going to rain?" you ask.

Continue on page 71.

"Is so," Tweedledum counters.

"It *isn't*." Tweedledee snaps the umbrella closed—with himself inside it and only his head sticking out.

"We don't have time to fight about this now," you tell them. "We're here to—"

Before you can finish the sentence and remind them of your mission, a huge wind whips up. The area grows so dark you can barely see the twins.

"Is it a storm?" you gasp, trying to keep your hair from blowing across your eyes. "*Inside* the castle?"

A loud *caw* startles you and you fall backward, knocking over the Tweedles. A gigantic crow swoops down and steals the rattle.

As you and the Tweedles try to untangle, there's another huge *whoosh* of wind as the crow returns. Only this time, what it steals is *you*!

It carries you in its beak to its nest built in one of the castle's tallest turrets. It drops you in with three squawking baby crows, then circles above you.

"They each get a worm for supper," the crow instructs you.

Continue on page 73.

The twins gaze up at the inside of the umbrella. "Not under here," Tweedledee says.

"Nor over *there*," Tweedledum chimes in, pointing to a spot next to them.

Suddenly, Tweedledum leaps forward, sending the umbrella flying. He grips your wrist.

"Do you see that?" he chokes out.

"That, being over there?" his brother adds, pointing toward a tangled collection of roots dead ahead.

You gesture for the Tweedles to move behind you. They do, clutching one another. You hold your breath as you cautiously move toward the roots. You can see something white poking up. Is it a bone? A *human* bone? You suppress a shudder.

You tentatively touch it with your foot. It rolls a bit, making little clicking sounds. You giggle with relief. "It's a rattle," you call back to the Tweedles.

You bend to pick it up, shaking off the dirt and leaves. "Not a rattle*snake*," you add, not wanting the twins to be frightened. "Only a child's toy rattle, quite old and broken." You turn and hold it out to them.

"I knew it was!" Tweedledum cries, stamping in a circle. He glares at his brother.

Tweedledee stomps back. "Contrariwise, you didn't. No-how!"

You gently lay your hand on Tweedledee's arm. "There, there. No need to be so angry about an old rattle."

"But it isn't old!" Tweedledee explodes.

YOU AND the Hatter creep deeper into the castle and climb the winding root stairway. You pass an open doorway and peek inside. Nothing but a large obsidian grandfather clock. "She has one, too!" you say, remembering the clock in Mirana's castle. "That's how she visits Time!"

You try another vegetation-covered door, and this one creaks open. Bottles of mysterious potions fill shelves on one wall. Easels covered with diagrams of the Chronosphere stand scattered throughout. On one table is a little flea circus and on another is an ant farm in an elaborate gold frame. A large rumpled bed stands in the corner, with hanging candles above it. Leaves are strewn across the dirt floor.

"These are Iracebeth's private chambers," you surmise, stepping inside.

Hatter looks around anxiously. "Father! Mother! Anyone?"

No response. You gaze around the room.

"They're not here," Hatter says. He sits down at one of the little tables, devastated. "I was certain they were here! I could feel it."

Continue on page 74.

"And don't let them stay up too late. It will make them cranky tomorrow."

"But—"

"Be sure they take turns with the rattle," the crow adds. "I won't be back too late." The crow gives each baby a peck on the head. "Be good," the bird tells them, then flies away.

Unbelievable. You set off to become a hero and wound up a babysitter! For birds!

You really didn't think this was how your day was going to . . .

END.

BABY CROWS AREN'T VERY INTERESTING
COMPANY. HEAD BACK TO PAGE 2 TO FIND
SOME OF YOUR MUCH MUCHIER FRIENDS.

You put a comforting hand on the Hatter's shoulder. Suddenly, he stands and picks up the ant farm. He holds it out to show you, smiling through his tears.

Your jaw drops. Inside the gilded frame, an outline of a hat is sketched in the sand!

You peer into the ant farm. It's not filled with ants—it's filled with tiny people! And from the Hatter's expression, you guess that you have found his family!

Boom! A massive gate falls over a window. *Boom! Boom! Boom!* Gates fall over *all* the windows. "We've got to get out of here!" you cry. The Hatter tucks the ant farm under his arm and you both spin around.

You gasp.

Iracebeth is blocking the doorway—your only means of escape.

She steps forward, smiling acidly. Four giant vegetable footmen hover behind her.

"Hello, *Alice!*" Her lips curl up in a nasty sneer.

She really hates me, you realize, growing cold. She has never forgiven you for defeating her Jabberwocky. When you did, the crown was returned to Mirana. And when Mirana's queenship was restored, she banished Iracebeth to this castle in the Outlands.

Iracebeth snaps her fingers. Two footmen step forward and seize you. She strolls over and slips her hand into your pocket. She yanks out the Chronosphere.

"Thank you ever so much!" she says. "You have delivered

to me the most powerful device in the entire Universe." She smiles smugly, then adds, "You've also delivered the person whom I hold truly responsible for all my suffering."

More vegetable footmen arrive, dragging all your friends with them. Your heart sinks. Your friends have been captured and are the Red Queen's prisoners.

"Now we shall see justice!" Iracebeth declares. She strides out, the guards forcing the others to follow.

You rush after her, but just as you reach the door, another massive gate falls in front of it. You struggle to squeeze through the bars, but you're too big. "Oh, Hatter," you cry, "what have I done? We have to stop her! We have to get out of here!"

"I have an idea!" Hatter exclaims.

A few minutes later the tiny Hightopps have been released from their ant farm prison and Zanik Hightopp sits inside a paper airplane—made from the little blue hat the Hatter gave his father all those years ago.

"I hope this works," you say, crossing your fingers for luck.

The Hatter throws the airplane through the bars on a window. Zanik pilots the little craft, screaming as he goes.

You hear thudding footfalls on the stairs. Then ripping, tearing, and snarling as something attacks the gate at the door. Terror sends tremors through you as you wonder, *Is this how it's going to end?*

"Hold on," you murmur. You recognize that snout, that spotted fur, those enormous jaws. . . . "The Bandersnatch!" you shout with glee.

"My plan worked!" the Hatter says, sounding a bit surprised.

With a furious snarl, the Bandersnatch rips apart the gate and uses its massive jaws to fling the broken pieces down the stairs. You're free!

The Hatter raises his hand and the Bandersnatch lowers his head. Zanik Hightopp leaps from the Bandersnatch's back onto the Hatter's palm.

"Now to grow you back . . ." the Hatter says.

You scan the room. "There!" you cry, pointing to a tea tray on a table. The Hatter lifts the dome from the covered plate and finds a tiny Upelkuchen cake. EAT ME is written in frosting across the top.

You and the Hatter break the cake into pieces and hand them around to the Hightopp family. They all return to their normal sizes—but not exactly dressed. You remember this problem from when *you* kept growing and shrinking. You quickly avert your eyes as they gather sheets, robes, and blankets to wrap themselves in.

Zanik and the Hatter reach out to hug each other, but something strange occurs: everything moves in slow motion for a moment, then returns to normal.

"What just happened?" you ask, puzzled.

The Hatter frowns. "I think it was a ripple in time."

That doesn't sound good.

Patches of rust appear in the cracks in the walls and floor.

You realize with horror what's going on. "Time!" you say. "He's slowing down. He's going to stop! It's why he wanted the Chronosphere so badly."

"Hang on!" the Hatter says, aghast. "If Time ends, we'll *all* end."

"This is my fault," you say. "I stole the Chronosphere from Time. And the Red Queen stole it from *me*!" You grow cold as you turn to the Hatter in dismay. "We have to get it back and return it to its rightful place!"

<hr />

You and the Hatter sneak along a corridor in the castle. "Where is everybody?" you whisper.

The Hatter peeks around a corner. "Look!" He points through an archway to a formal garden. Iracebeth stands in front of a queen's throne and wields a judge's gavel. Time slumps in the king's throne beside her, clutching his heart.

"Time doesn't look very good," you say as you and the Hatter sneak behind some topiaries. "I can barely hear him ticking."

Mirana stands in front of the thrones, bound. McTwisp stands next to her, peering through spectacles at a sheaf of papers. The rest of your friends are being guarded by giant vegetable footmen.

"What's going on?" you whisper.

Iracebeth points her gavel at her sister, the White Queen. "Mirana of Marmoreal," she bellows, "you are accused of treason! I hereby sentence you to . . ."

You gasp. "It's a trial!"

"What are the charges against me?" Mirana asks.

"You have lied!" Iracebeth screams in her sister's face. "You have stolen. You are *not* the rightful queen of Underland."

"Objection!" McTwisp calls out. "Where's your proof?"

Iracebeth spins in a fury, lifting the Chronosphere. "I don't need proof! I've got better! I shall have a confession!"

She glares at Mirana, who shrinks back. *She's nervous,* you realize. As if maybe there really *is* something to confess. Something she did in the past.

Curiouser and curiouser.

Before you can ask the Hatter if he knows of anything Mirana may have done, Iracebeth throws the Chronosphere to the ground. It opens to full size, ready for travel.

You burst from your hiding place and run into the garden. "Wait! Stop! Wait!"

Everyone gapes at you. You know what Iracebeth is trying to do, and you have to stop it. "You cannot change the past," you tell her. "Believe me, I have tried."

Iracebeth just rolls her eyes, then grabs Mirana and yanks her into the Chronosphere. It takes off, flying into the sky and disappearing.

Hatter runs up to join you. You grip his arms. "We've got to stop her!" you cry.

Vegetable footmen approach you and Hatter, and they sure don't look as if they're about to offer you tea. Never have an asparagus man and a cabbage-headed servant looked so menacing.

Suddenly, an enormous roar stops everyone in their tracks. The Bandersnatch, carrying the Hightopp family, gleefully bounds up to you and the Hatter.

Using the distraction, you race over to Time. You and the Hatter quickly untie him while the Hightopps lay out pieces of the partially reassembled time machine.

Rust is spreading over Time's body. "Please," you beg as you shake him, trying to rouse him. "Please wake up." He stirs and gives a little moan.

"You've got to take us back," you say as his eyes flicker open. "The Red Queen! She's going to change the past!"

"I'm too weak," Time moans.

"No, you're not," you say. "You're Time. The infinite."

"The immortal!" the Hatter adds. He points at his family, who are trying to put together the pieces of the machine. "Besides, you're the only person who can rebuild that thing!"

Time's eyes flick to where Hatter is pointing. They widen

at the sight of the machinery the Hightopps have laid out. "The Tempus Fugit!" he says. He turns back to you and the Hatter and grins.

You have a feeling he's on your side now.

⁓

As you fly across the Ocean of Time, you see that all the past days are now flecked with patches of rust. You give Time a quick glance. He looks dismayed. That's not very encouraging.

"There they are!" the Hatter cries. "The Big Head and Mirana! Hurry!"

You spot the two queens in the Chronosphere up ahead. Time has nearly caught up to it when it suddenly veers downward, disappearing into an image you recognize. The snowy night that changed Underland forever. Fell Day.

"Why would Big Head come here?" Hatter wonders.

"Something happened when they were young girls," you say. "And she's going to try to stop it. To change the past."

"That's not the worst danger," Time says, sounding weak. "If their past selves see their present selves, well . . . let's just say that better not happen."

Your brain reels as you try to figure out how to prevent that. Distracted, you land the Tempus Fugit suddenly and roughly. You leap out of the vehicle and see that Iracebeth and Mirana are heading straight toward the room they shared as little girls! And then something strange happens. They stop and actually embrace! Does this mean they've declared a truce? A grin spreads across your face. That would be wonderful! Not just for the queens but for all of Underland.

But then the bedroom door opens. Little Iracebeth stands in the doorway. Her eyes travel up to grown-up Iracebeth's giant head. She lets out a piercing shriek!

FWOMP! Both Iracebeths freeze, turning into rust-covered statues. Rust begins to spread outward from where they stand.

"Oh, this can't be good," the Hatter pronounces.

"She has broken the past," Time says weakly. "We've got to get to the Grand Clock before it stops forever."

Your crash landing totaled the Tempus Fugit, so you've got to get everyone into the Chronosphere. "Hurry, *hurry!*" you urge.

Mirana drags her rust-frozen sister into the glowing bands while Hatter maneuvers the weakened Time into position. You take your place at the controls. In only a moment, you're traveling across the Ocean of Time once more. Below you, rust spreads across the land, freezing everything it touches.

Your experience at sea serves you well. You expertly pilot the Chronosphere across the Ocean of Time toward the present.

"The rust!" Hatter cries. "It's catching up!"

You glance over your shoulder. The rust is like a wave coming after you.

You bite your lip, concentrating. You've never traveled at such a speed—and with so much at stake.

You reach the castle and zip through the doorway. The Chronosphere shoots through the vast hall as floors, ceilings, and walls rust and crumble around you.

You zoom up the root staircase as an enormous wave rushes through the castle doors. It splits into two powerful, pounding waves, swallowing everything behind you.

The Chronosphere ricochets off the rusting walls as you steer it along collapsing corridors. As the castle breaks apart, you see rust clouds falling from the sky. All of Underland is going to freeze into a rust-covered wasteland if you don't get the Chronosphere back where it belongs! You force yourself to ignore the shattering, rusting world around you.

"I've really enjoyed our time together, Alice," the Hatter says somberly.

You stay laser-focused on your destination. You'll use Iracebeth's grandfather clock to get to Time's castle, just as she did for their date.

You expertly maneuver the Chronosphere into the giant grandfather clock at breakneck speed, the waves roaring behind you. You emerge in the Chamber of the Grand Clock in Time's castle, where the Chronosphere crashes to the floor. You, Hatter, Mirana, the rust-frozen Iracebeth, and Time tumble out. The Chronosphere collapses back to its small size.

You grab it. The Grand Clock of All Time is barely ticking. It's running out of time, and so are you.

The rust is even worse here. You have to dodge through the deluge. Rusted Seconds, Minutes, and an Hour lie scattered across the floor, motionless.

"Time has collapsed!" Hatter calls out behind you.

You gape at the Grand Clock. It ticks one last tock and then stops.

The way you see it, you have two options—neither promising. . . .

RUN AS FAST AS YOU CAN
AND TURN TO PAGE 86.

OR THROW THE CHRONOSPHERE
AS HARD AS POSSIBLE, GO TO PAGE 85,
AND FLIP THE BOOK.

YOU'LL NEVER make it in time. Rust creeps closer and closer, moving faster and faster. You fling the Chronosphere with all your might, hoping you aimed well.

Your aim was fine—but you didn't know your own strength. The Chronosphere crashes through the clock and smashes into the wall behind it! It breaks into thousands of pieces, splintering time itself!

Every single moment of the past and present for everyone in the room appears. You as an infant, crawling around and getting into everything, because you are quite curious about things, even at this young age. You as a precocious little girl. You as a great-great-grandma, spry as ever.

It's so noisy! And crowded! You try to find your way out but it's a labyrinth of multiple Alices going on forever!

This time there is no

END.

THERE ARE TOO MANY ALICES! GOOD THING YOU
CAN GO BACK TO PAGE 2 AND BE SOMEONE ELSE.

YOU RUN as fast as you can. The rust is nearly upon you, creeping up your heels, your feet, your waist. You slam the Chronosphere back where it belongs as the rust spreads across your hand.

You're frozen in a terrible silence. Everything in the room, the castle, the world—all trapped in rust. Were you too late?

Then—the smallest of *ticks. Ticktock. TICKTOCK.*

Deep within the rusted clock, the Chronosphere glows and starts to hum. There's a crackling sound as the machinery seems to shrug off the rust and start up again.

Slowly, the rust begins to recede.

You watch as the skies clear and color returns to the world outside the windows.

Mirana, the Hatter, Iracebeth—unfrozen, though dazed—gaze all around as the rust dissolves.

You hurry over to Time. "Are you all right?"

Time looks at you with grateful eyes and nods.

There's a commotion in the hallway, then McTwisp, Mally, the Tweedles, and the Hightopps pour into the room.

Happy tears spring to your eyes as you enjoy the reunions

taking place. The Hatter and his family. Mirana and Iracebeth getting along, perhaps for the first time since they were little girls.

"I owe you an apology," you tell Time. "You tried to warn me about the Chronosphere, but I didn't listen."

"No worries, my dear," Time says kindly. "I heal all wounds."

"You know, I used to think you were a thief, stealing everything I loved," you admit. "But you give before you take. And every day is a gift. Every hour, every minute, every second . . ."

You reach into your pocket and retrieve your father's broken pocket watch, then gaze down at it.

"Ah, the fallen soldier," Time says. "I suppose you want me to fix it."

You study the watch.

IF YOU WANT TIME TO FIX IT,
TURN TO PAGE 89 AND FLIP THE BOOK.

IF YOU WANT TO GIVE IT
TO TIME AS A GIFT, TURN TO PAGE 90.

BUT WHAT FUN IS IT TO HEAR A STORY WHEN
YOU CAN LIVE IT? HEAD BACK TO PAGE 2 AND
CHOOSE A NEW TALE TO BE A PART OF.

YOU GIVE Time the watch to repair. When he hands it back to you, there's a blinding flash of light.

You blink a few times and shade your eyes with your hands. "Where is he?" you say, searching the riverbank for your friend.

Your sister sits in the bow of the boat. "Do be patient, Alice," she says. "You're acting like a complete baby and you are already a big girl of seven! Just enjoy the lovely sunny day."

You settle in your seat in the rowboat. "Well, when father's friend does finally arrive," you say, "he's going to have to tell us an especially good story."

Your sister dips her hand in the water and splashes you. "Professor Charles Dodgson always tells a good story."

You splash her back. "True. But I think this time it's going to have to be all about me!" you declare. "About all the adventures I will have. Adventures that will never come to

an

END."

"N O," YOU say, holding the watch out to him. "I want you to have it."

Time looks surprised. "You said it was your father's."

"It *was* my father's," you say, gazing down at it. Then you look up at Time and smile. "But it's not my *father*."

You look around at all the happy families. "I've been holding on too tightly to all the wrong things."

Time gives you a little bow, then tucks the watch into his pocket. "My dear girl. They say I am a friend to no man. But I shall remember you. Always."

The Hatter approaches you and excitedly grabs your hand. "We did it, didn't we?"

"We did indeed." You fling your arms around him in a tight hug. "And I think it's time for me to go home."

He pats your back. "Don't worry, Alice. In the palace of dreams we shall meet, and laugh, and play all our lives."

"But a dream is not reality," you say, your voice breaking a little.

He takes your hands and brings his face close to yours,

his eyes shining madly. "Ah, but who's to say which is which?"

You smile through your tears and nod.

⌒⌒⌒

You arrive in Hamish's mansion. A meeting is taking place in the library. You stand outside the doorway, listening to Hamish pressuring your mother to sign the papers that will give him control of the *Wonder.*

"Let's get this over with," you hear Hamish say. "Time is money."

That's a cue if you ever heard one. You step into the library. "He most certainly is not!" you declare.

They all turn and stare at you. Hamish, Lady Ascot, Mr. Harcourt, and your mother.

You stroll around the table until you reach your mother's chair. "Sign the papers, Mother." You pick the pen up from the desk and hand it to her.

She doesn't move to take it. "But what about your dreams?" she asks.

You sit beside her. "I used to think the *Wonder* meant everything, but it's just a ship. There is always another ship. But you and your well-being mean everything to me. You're my mother and I only get one."

Her eyes grow shiny with tears. You both stand and stroll out of the library, arm in arm, ignoring the sputtering Hamish behind you.

A few months later you watch a pair of workmen installing a sign above your office door: KINGSLEIGH AND KINGSLEIGH TRADING COMPANY. You smile with satisfaction.

Beside you, Mr. Harcourt, Hamish's *former* clerk, studies papers on a clipboard. "A full cargo aboard," he tells you. He holds the clipboard against his chest and grins. "Do we commence with Kingsleigh and Kingsleigh's maiden voyage?"

"Best check with the commodore," you tell him.

You cross the wharf of the bustling Hong Kong harbor and stroll to a graceful ship, loaded and ready to push off.

Your mother greets you with a quick hug.

"Ready to head out of harbor, Commodore?" you ask her.

She nods with a broad smile. "Full sail, lads!" she calls out. "Full sail!"

You gaze at the harbor teeming with boats. You grip the rigging and relish the feel of the wind in your hair, the waves beneath your feet. You're ready for your new adventure!

This is not

THE END—

it's just the beginning!

YOU'VE FOUND A NEW LIFE FULL OF SEAFARING EXCITEMENT, BUT THERE ARE STILL ADVENTURES TO BE HAD IN UNDERLAND IF YOU TURN BACK TO PAGE 2.

THE HATTER

YOU PLOP the third hat on top of your head. It's the one you got for your eighth birthday three weeks ago. You proudly walk out of the house, balancing the hats very well, if you do say so yourself.

Chessur, the little Cheshire Kitten; puppy Bayard; and your friends the twins Tweedledum and Tweedledee run by. You chase after them, gleefully stomping in puddles. You scoop up some muddy water with your school satchel and splash the twins. Your tower of hats tumbles off your head as you leap from puddle to puddle.

You hear your father calling your name. Uh-oh. He doesn't sound happy. You turn to see him glaring at you from the doorway.

Your eyes flick from his scowling face to your smiling friends.

Decisions, decisions.

When you turn to glance back at your father, you spot a young lady watching you.

SHOULD YOU KEEP PLAYING WITH YOUR FRIENDS?
THEN TURN TO PAGE 99 AND FLIP THE BOOK.

OR SHOULD YOU BRING THE YOUNG LADY INTO
YOUR FATHER'S HAT SHOP? TURN TO PAGE 100.

But finding Chessur isn't easy! You think you catch sight of him when you see four paws scampering down an alley. You run after them.

Now you see a tail and a little kitty butt. Suddenly, the butt falls backward, landing right on its tail. You rush over as Chessur's body gradually comes into view.

"Are you okay?" you ask.

"I don't know what happened," he mews plaintively.

"You need to remember to at least make your eyes appear if you're going to go running around," you tell him. You stroke his soft aqua-and-gray-striped fur.

A loud sound startles you, making your head whip around. "Just a Jubjub bird," you say, turning to look at Chess. But his face has disappeared. "Why, Chess, I believe you've lost your head!"

His face reappears but now his body vanishes. "Found it," he purrs.

Maybe you'd better not take disappearing lessons from him. At least not until he has it under control. You'd hate to get stuck with invisible limbs.

You spend the rest of the afternoon playing all kinds of games with Chess and having a lovely time in

THE END.

Continue on page 101.

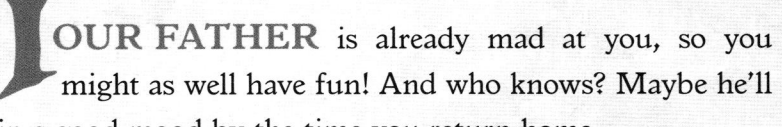

YOUR FATHER is already mad at you, so you might as well have fun! And who knows? Maybe he'll be in a good mood by the time you return home.

You run off with Bayard and the Tweedles. The Cheshire Kitten seems to have vanished. You're not worried, though. That's just the kind of kitty he is—the disappearing kind!

Bayard picks up a stick and tosses it. You bound after it on all fours. You snatch it up in your mouth and gleefully waggle it. The Tweedles jump up and down, clapping with delight. Suddenly, Bayard's nose sticks straight up in the air and twitches. "Gotta go!" he says, tail wagging. "Sniffed out a delicious scent."

He lopes away, leaving you with Tweedledum and Tweedledee. They're taking turns bonking each other on the head and giggling madly.

You decide to leave them to their game to go find Chessur. Maybe he can teach you how to disappear. That trick would come in handy. Especially on days like today, when your father is a big ol' grump.

BRINGING IN a customer might please your father. Then maybe he'll be less likely to scold you. The pretty lady is smiling at you, so you march over to her and grab her hand. She looks surprised but goes with you into the shop.

"We're closed," your father says gruffly. You glance up at the lady, hoping she isn't frightened by your father's tone. He is such a serious sourpuss sometimes.

"Papa! Look!" you say, holding up the lady's hand in yours. "A customer with a lovely head. Right here!"

"I'm sorry, miss." Your father stands and puts on his coat. He means business. That's nothing new. He *always* means business. "You'll have to come another time."

Maybe the lady won't be getting a new hat now, but you have one to show your father. You follow him to the door and tug on his coat.

"Papa, look! I made something for you in school!" You open your puddle-spattered satchel and proudly hold up a little blue hat made from construction paper.

Continue on page 102.

BUT AFTER AN AFTERNOON OF PLAYING,
CHESS TAKES AN INVISIBLE CATNAP AND
YOU CAN'T FIND ANY OF HIM ANYWHERE.
GO BACK TO PAGE 2 AND SEE IF YOU
CAN FIND MORE OF YOUR FRIENDS.

Your father peers down. "What is it?"

Is he losing his eyesight? "A hat!" you say.

He takes it from you. "This? Let me have a look. . . ." He starts to take the construction paper hat apart.

"But—" you protest.

"If my son is going to make a hat, he will make a proper one," your father says. "Do something, do it right—that's my philosophy." He fiddles with the hat, his big fingers tearing it.

You gasp. He's ruining it!

"Hmmm. Well, cheap material," your father says. "There's your lesson. Tell you what . . . tomorrow I'll help you make a real hat, Son. Not one of these pretend ones, eh?"

You watch, stunned, as your father crinkles up the hat and tosses it into the trash. Then he walks out of the shop.

You gape after him, tears springing to your eyes. He makes you so mad! You furiously swipe at the tears. You don't want to be here anymore. That'll show him!

Where should you go? Or maybe a better question is, *when* should you go?

IF YOU WANT TO REVISIT A MOMENT IN THE PAST,
GO TO PAGE 103 AND FLIP THE BOOK.

IF YOU WANT TO SKIP AHEAD INTO THE FUTURE,
TURN TO PAGE 104.

YOU DECIDE to go three weeks into the past: back to your eighth birthday party. That was a *frabjous* day!

All your friends sit around the festive party table. You take turns eating and drinking the special cakes and potions that make you grow smaller or larger. You laugh hysterically when Mallymkun the Dormouse eats so much Upelkuchen cake she can reach in through your bedroom window on the second floor and get six more hats for you and your friends.

After many giddy experiments, you and your friends settle on your perfect sizes for the afternoon. You clap your hands and declare, "Time for Stick the Swizzle on Chessur!"

This is much harder than it sounds, since different parts of the kitty keep vanishing! You twirl around blindfolded, then stumble to where you hear Chessur purring. You whip off the blindfold, confident that you won!

Oops! As Chessur materializes, you realize that you stuck the striped candy right on his nose! Everyone laughs—Chess the hardest of all.

You have so much fun that you return to this day over

Continue on page 105.

MAYBE THINGS will be better when you're older. You go into the future and arrive on Toomalie Day—the day of the coronation. Your father had the great honor of making the tiaras for the princesses. You're now in your twenties and quite an accomplished hatter apprentice to your father.

You stand with him in the throne room of Witzend Castle, holding hatboxes. You're a little nervous. Every citizen of Witzend is there to witness the great event.

Mirana looks lovely dressed all in white. Iracebeth, on the other hand . . . she must have a headache in that over-sized head of hers, because she hasn't smiled once. You don't particularly like being this close to her. She's a nasty piece of work, that one.

Your father has just placed the tiara on Mirana's head and is reaching out his hand to you. You quickly open a hatbox and pull out Iracebeth's tiara. It's much bigger and heavier than Mirana's. You hope you don't drop it!

You give it to your father. But when he tries to put it on Iracebeth's head, it doesn't fit.

Continue on page 106.

and over again. The best parts are that your father is always in a good mood and you never run out of cake!

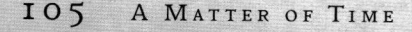

THE END

AH, BUT EVENTUALLY YOU DO RUN OUT OF
ROOM IN YOUR STOMACH FOR CAKE. GO BACK
TO PAGE 2 TO TRY A DIFFERENT PATH.

You can't help yourself: you chuckle.

You can see Iracebeth is growing impatient. Your father tries again, pushing down on the tiara harder. Iracebeth tugs on it, too.

You laugh again, and this time there are snickers in the crowd. Your father and Iracebeth yank on the tiara so hard it breaks in two, sending jewels flying. The whole room guffaws.

Irate, Iracebeth points a trembling finger at your father. You don't believe it! Her head grows even larger! Rage must be making it expand.

"Zanik Hightopp!" she bellows. "I will never forget what you and your family have done to me this day!"

She yells and screams at everyone, but all you can see is your father's furious expression—directed at *you*. He's so angry you worry that *his* head will swell up like Iracebeth's. When Iracebeth storms off the stage, your father turns on you.

"All I did was laugh, Father!" you say in your defense. "I couldn't help it."

You and your father argue, the way you always do. "Why am I never good enough for you?" you finally ask, throwing up your hands.

"Why are you always such a disappointment to me?" he demands at the same time.

Your arms fall to your sides. It takes enormous effort, but you keep yourself under control. No tears. No shouts. You speak very reasonably. "There. You've said it. Well, if I'm such a disappointment, I don't suppose you'll be sorry if I leave home!"

Your mother rushes up and grabs your father's arm. "Tarrant, no!" she begs you. She looks pleadingly up at your father. "Please, Zanik, tell him to stay! Zanik!"

Your father straightens up even taller. "If he is to be a hatter worthy of the Hightopp name, he must be sane, sober, disciplined, prudent, punctual, punctilious." He shakes off your mother's arm and points at you. "Everything he is now *not*!"

How can you be all those things? Where is the fun in any of that?

You fear if you say anything, you'll get into a screaming match with him, or, worse, not be able to fight the tears welling in your eyes. You give your mother a sad nod, then stride out of the throne room.

You march along Witzend Street. You're hurt, angry, and confused.

You hear someone calling your name.

You turn and see a young blond woman rushing toward you. To your utter shock, she throws her arms around you.

"It's you, isn't it? It's really you!" she cries.

Startled, you stumble backward a bit. Righting yourself, you say, "I'm sorry. Have we met?"

She releases you and grins. "Yes! I mean, no! I mean, not yet." She laughs and shakes her head. "I'm Alice."

You cock your head and study her. She *does* seem familiar,

in an entirely unfamiliar way. "Funny. I feel I should know you."

A passing merchant carries a large basket of ribbons. You lift a particularly luscious blue one from the pile and start walking. You want to put some distance between you and the castle. You don't want your father to come across you on the street and start berating you again.

"We met once, when I was young," the woman explains, walking beside you. "Years from now. When you're older."

"So you're Alice, my new, old friend." You grin at her. "You're bonkers, aren't you?"

"Am I?" she asks.

"All the best ones are," you assure her.

You and your new, old friend walk by a fruit stand. You quickly snag a purplemelon fruit. A hat is beginning to take form in your mind, and when that happens, your hands must follow.

"You must meet my friend Thackery Earwicket," you say. You spot a borogrove sunning itself in a window. You yank out a few of its colorful tail feathers.

"*Squarrk!*" the bird complains, and snaps its beak at you. You tip your hat at it, hoping the gesture will suffice as both a thank-you and an apology.

"Ol' Thackery lives out by the old mill," you tell Alice. "I'm hoping he'll put me up for a bit. Will you join us for tea?"

You stop walking so you can flick, fluff, and finalize your

creation. With a flourish you produce for Alice a delightfully deranged hat, purple and blue with white feathers. Delighted, she puts it on. You pull a mirror from your pocket so she can admire your creation.

You resume your pleasant amble and come to a large oak tree. You crook your finger so Alice will move closer to you. "Can you keep a secret?" you whisper. "This tree is magical! Every night when I was a boy I would make a wish, and the next morning the tree would have granted it. Usually green-and-white Swizzles." You lick your lips, remembering. "Delicious!" You give the tree a fond pat. "What a tree!"

You walk on, assuming Alice will follow.

Instead, she has stopped and calls after you. "Wait! Stop! Your family is in danger! You must warn them about Horunvendush Day!"

You turn and stare at her. Is this some kind of trick? "I've no idea what you're talking about, but if my father sent you to change my mind, you can tell him that I never will."

Seething, you spin around and stalk away.

"Tarrant, wait!" she shouts. "Listen! You are right now creating a past you will never be able to change. Hatter!"

You stick your fingers in your ears and ignore her. You thought she was your friend, not a spy for your father!

You can't talk about this right now. The wound is too fresh. You pick up your pace. Only, where should you go?

GO TO PAGE 112 AND MARCH
FURIOUSLY TO THE MARCH HARE'S HOUSE.

OR GO FARTHER INTO THE FUTURE BY
JUMPING TO PAGE 111 AND FLIPPING THE BOOK.

YOU GO far into the future. But something is wrong. You can't put your finger on it at first. Then it comes to you.

"No hats?" No matter where you look, there is not a single, solitary hatted head. They're all bare. With very elaborate hairstyles.

"Excuse me," you say to a girl with orange-and-purple-striped hair piled into a two-and-a-half-foot tower. "Where does one buy hats?"

"What's *haaa-wt*?" she asks, pronouncing the word as if it were a foreign language.

You clutch your heart. Can it be true? A world without hats?

You wander the streets, confused and sad. You pass the place where your father's hat shop once stood. It's now a hair salon, famous for creating the tallest designs in all of Underland.

You stand in front of the salon and raise your fist to the

Continue on page 113.

YOU SIT at a festively decorated table. Glum, you slump in a chair. Mallymkun, the Dormouse, lifts a teaspoon as big as she is and slides it onto a saucer. Thackery hops about in typical March Hare fashion, putting finishing touches on the table settings.

"Teatime!" Thackery says, bouncing over to you and carrying a plate piled with scones.

"Cheer up, Tarrant," Mally says, sitting beside your plate. "We'll have fun now that you're living here."

A bizarre sound makes you look at the sky. The Universe itself seems to tear open, and an extraordinary machine careens through. Its pilot is even more astonishing. Clad in blacks and silvers, this new arrival is tall, with an impressive mustache and shoulder pads as wide as the March Hare's height. And oh, what a hat! He smashes into the windmill sails, then crash-lands in a crumpled heap.

Your eyebrow lifts. *This could be interesting,* you think. A bit mad, as a matter of fact. You inhale deeply. Yes, you definitely detect a whiff of nuttiness. Perhaps things are about to improve?

Continue on page 114.

sky. "It may take the rest of my life, but I will make it my mission to bring the hat back to Underland!" you swear.

Now that you have a goal, you have renewed vigor. You create the very first hat museum, hoping that will kindle interest in the citizens. Only problem is there are no hats to put on display. So you set about making them. You work day and night and day and night and day and night and day and night and eventually become known as that crazy curmudgeon always talking about the good old days. Mostly people just call you the Mad Hatter.

THE END

LIVING IN A PLACE WITHOUT HATS IS JUST
TOO HORRIFYING. FLIP BACK TO PAGE 2
TO GO ON A DIFFERENT ADVENTURE.

The unusual fellow grunts and groans as he extricates himself from his flying device. Seems a bit rickety for a fellow of his proportions, but if he wants to risk it . . .

"Greetings. I am Time," he announces. "The infinite and immortal. You may express your awe and wonder. But keep it short."

Mally bows. She nudges Thackery. He bows, too. But you don't. This fellow irks you. You don't like it when someone takes your awe for granted.

"I wonder, my lord," you say, "why you have lowered yourself to mingle amongst us mere and mundane mortals?"

He looks a little shifty. "Ah, well. I'm looking for a girl called Alice. Have you seen her?"

Alice? That's the new old friend you just met for the first time again. You eye him suspiciously. "What is your business with her?"

"She took something from me. I need it back. As soon as possible."

Hmmm. She didn't strike you as a thief. You need to find out more. "You're in luck, oh, eternal one!" you say. "Why, just today I invited Alice to tea. Have a seat! We can wait together!"

Mally and Thackery look at you in surprise. You signal to them with your eyes to play along. They shrug as Time sits.

"If you're really Time itself, or *him*self," you say, sloshing some tea into his cup, "perhaps you can answer me this. I've always wondered when 'soon' is. Is it before 'in a few minutes' or after 'a little while'?" You grin at him and offer up a plate. "Scone?"

Time studies you disdainfully. "If you vex me, it'll be an eternity."

You continue your interrogation of Time. "Is it true you heal all wounds?" You grab a butter knife to test this theory. You reach for Thackery's ear, but he bounds away, knocking you backward. The knife skitters along the table.

Mallymkun scurries up to Time. "We have such a *lovely* Time here!" she says. She pats his cheek with her tiny paw and bats her eyelashes at him flirtatiously.

"The best Time ever!" Thackery agrees, giving Time a thumping whack on the back.

You stretch out on top of the table, belly down. You prop yourself up on your elbows, resting your chin in your hands.

"Do you fly when you're having fun?" You cock your head to the right. "And why is it that you wait for no man? Do you wait for women?" You pop up onto all fours. "For animals?"

Time stands and glowers down at you. "Bah!" he growls, giving you a dismissive wave of his hand. He turns and stomps away.

You follow Time and put your hands on his head. "Look! I've got Time on my hands!"

He smacks your hands away and keeps walking.

Mally runs up beside Time. "Yes, but Time is on my side!"

You dash to the table and pour tea into a cup. Then you race back to Time and hold the teacup up to him. "Oh, oh! Now I'm serving Time!"

Thackery flops onto the ground, laughing hysterically.

"I'm racing against Time!" you shout, starting to run. Time has much longer legs than you, so when he picks up speed, you have to jog to keep up with him.

Mally scrambles up your leg and perches on your shoulder. She takes out her tiny sword and wallops Time with the hilt over and over. "I'm beating Time!" she chortles.

"I'm passing Time!" you cheer, pulling ahead of him.

Mally flips around her sword and aims its tip at Time's throat. "I'm killing Time!" Mally declares.

You quickly flick Mally's sword out of her hand. "I'm saving Time!" you say, then waggle a finger disapprovingly at Mally. She wiggles her whiskers at you and jumps off your shoulder.

She lands beside Thackery, who hoots and hollers, thumping the ground with his oversized feet and rolling around on the grass.

You grab Time's arms and flap them up and down. "Look, look! Time is flying! No, no, wait!" You knock Time onto the ground. As he gets up on all fours, you leap onto his back. "Time is crawling!" you shout.

Time flings you off him and stands up abruptly.

"Enough!" Time bellows. "Stop! *Please!*"

You look at him.

DO YOU CONTINUE TEASING HIM?
THEN GO TO PAGE 120 AND KEEP READING.

OR DO YOU STOP?
GO TO PAGE 119 AND FLIP THE BOOK.

REALLY? STOP making jokes? You *must* be mad! Are you sure you're Tarrant Hightopp, the Mad Hatter? Positive?

Then you'd better make a different choice. Because there's no way the *real* Hatter would ever choose to stop his shenanigans.

So turn this book right side up again and go to page 120 if you want anyone to believe you're the Hatter!

THE END

YOU SLING an arm across Time's shoulder. "Tell me, old bean. Do you exist at all? Some say Time is an illusion."

Time shakes off your arm. "I am not an illusion! Could an illusion do this?"

You watch as Time reaches into his heart clock and stops the second hand. The entire world freezes. The tea from the pot hangs in the air, mid-pour. Mally's tongue is reaching to lick a sugar cube, and Thackery's mouth is wide open as he's stopped in the middle of a guffaw. Only you and Time can move.

"Without me there is nothing," Time declares. "If you were to die, no one would care. But if Time were to stop, this world would end!"

You pop your head under the stalled tea, examining it. "Actually, quite impressive . . ."

Time resumes. The tea pours onto your face, soaking you. You stand back up and look at Time. He's breathing heavily and looks a bit worn out.

"Now, when is Alice coming?" he asks.

You pull out a chair and sit. You mop your face with the tablecloth, then tip back your chair and put your feet up on the table, crossing them at the ankles. "I never said she was, old bean! I merely said I invited her."

"*What?* You, you—" Time gets himself back under control. "Nicely done, sir. But now it's my turn. You were asking when Now is?"

Time looms over you. He opens his cloak to reveal his heart clock. It shows 5:59 p.m. Suddenly, you're not so sure of yourself. What's the blighter up to?

"*Now* is precisely one minute to teatime," Time declares. "And until Alice joins you for tea, it will *always* be one minute to teatime." He sneers at you. "Enjoy your little party." Time moves the clock in his chest backward and disappears.

"Well, that was entertaining," you say. "But now I think I'd like a bit of that pretty little pink cake." You move to push up from your seat, only you can't. You try to stand. You grunt, you strain, you struggle, but no matter what you do, you can't get up!

"Say, old chappies." You keep your voice light, not wanting to alarm them. "Are you in any way troubled by a wee lack of mobility?"

Mallymkun and Thackery wiggle their whiskers at each other in confusion. "Speak plain," Mally says.

"Can you get up?" you say.

Thackery snorts. "Why, of course I—" A puzzled

expression appears on his furry face. "That is to say I—" He gives Mally a worried look.

Frowning, the Dormouse tries to move. "Uh-oh . . ." she whispers.

All three of you try to get up with great effort: you break into a sweat, Thackery's floppy ears stand straight up, and Mally's eyes bug out. But none of you can move. Not an inch!

"What's he done?" Mally squeaks.

"The blighter's stuck us all at one minute to teatime!" You'd slam the table if you could pick up your arm. "Slurking-sluvishurksum!"

You eye the delicious spread Thackery and Mally have laid out for tea. "Time is a cruel one," you say bitterly. This is worse than if you'd stayed at home and listened to your father's scolding all day long!

Mally sighs. "We'll never get to have any of this! It will all spoil!"

"Spare the rod and spoil the tea," the March Hare intones.

"What the blazes does that mean?" you ask. You can't even turn your head to glare at him. How frustrating.

"How should I know? I'm as mad as you are, remember?" Thackery replies.

You have no idea if days are passing, since the entire world around the table is frozen with you. No sunrises, no sunsets. Just loooong stretches to fill. Luckily, Mally and Thackery are two of your favorite people. Though just now Mallymkun is fast asleep and Thackery is trying to count how many different faces he can make. Not very entertaining.

Then a figure appears on the horizon. As it approaches, you can make out a hatless head sprouting long blond hair. A dress with a pinafore. "It's a little girl!" you say. She looks to be about seven or eight years old.

"Hello," she says as she reaches the table. "Are you having a tea party?"

"Would you like to join us?" you ask.

"Why, yes, thank you," she says. "I'm feeling a bit peckish."

You hold your breath to see what will happen when she sits down. Will she also be trapped at one minute till teatime?

She lowers herself into the plush armchair at the head of the table. *Don't get too excited,* you tell yourself. *The big test will be if she can get up again!*

"Excuse me, dearie," you say. "Would you mind terribly passing the butter?"

She picks up the butter dish and then—*gasp!*—she gets up and brings it to you. "This is a terribly long table," she remarks, putting the butter dish down in front of you. "It must make passing dishes rather tiresome."

You blink rapidly. Can it be true? Can you actually move? More important, will it *finally* be teatime? You keep your eyes on her face as you reach for your teacup. There's something very familiar about her.

"Yes!" You practically chortle with joy. The teacup is at your lips. You managed to lift it from the saucer! And now you are going to have your tea, because it is, after all this time, *teatime*!

"Gah!" You spit out the tea. It's been sitting in the cup for who knows how long. Not only is it cold, but twigs and insects have fallen into it, and cobwebs crisscross the top.

"Wh-wh-what?" Mally sputters awake. She shakes her head and narrows her eyes at the guest. "Who's that?"

You realize what has happened. "She's Alice!" you cry. "Time said it would stay one minute to teatime until Alice joined us. Then this girl arrives and it is finally no longer one minute until teatime! It is the very time of tea itself!"

You fling yourself back against your chair, proud of your deductive skills. "That was rather well done, don't you think, Alice?"

"You know my name?" Alice asks.

You wave a hand at her. "We've met. But you were older."

She just stares at you.

"Never mind, never mind," you say.

Suddenly, Thackery bounds onto the table, scattering dishes and spilling the milk jug. "Free!" he shouts. He twirls around, his ears flapping. "Time is on the move again!"

Speaking of moving—now that you can, what do you want to do?

DO YOU WANT TO TRY TO FIND SOMETHING
EDIBLE ON THE FAR SIDE OF THE TABLE?
TURN TO PAGE 127 AND FLIP THE BOOK.

OR SHOULD YOU TAKE ADVANTAGE OF YOUR
NEWLY RETURNED MOBILITY AND GO
SOMEWHERE—ANYWHERE? TURN TO PAGE 128.

"Oh! Yes!" She pulls a huge slice of cake from one pinafore pocket and a shiny blue bottle from the other. You accept the cake.

You're about to take a bite when you remember your manners. "May I?" you ask her.

"Please do," she says politely.

You take a big bite. You grow and grow until your head pokes through the trees. Startled birds caw angrily at you and fly off.

One problem: now that you're up here, how do you reach the bottle that will shrink you back down?

Hmmm. Perhaps you didn't think this all the way through.

"Halllooooo down there!" you call. "A little help, please!"

You think maybe you hear Thackery and Mallymkun shouting up to you, but you're not entirely sure. It's pretty windy above the tree line.

You scan the nearby trees, hoping perhaps a friendly bird could bring your friends a message. But all you see are those nasty Jubjub birds. They'd peck your nose before they'd ever agree to being helpful!

Continue on page 129.

YOU STRETCH out a bit, then stroll to the far side of the table and grab some biscuits. It feels delightful to be back on your feet again, but you're very curious about the child version of the Alice you met. You'd like to stay here to learn more about her. So you skip back to her spot at the table. You wonder what she could possibly have taken from Time. His favorite hat, perhaps?

"Tell me, dearie," you say. "How have you been spending your time?"

"It's been very confusing, actually," she admits. "I've been so many different sizes today, I hardly know myself!"

"Lovely!" you say. You are now in the best mood ever. Everything is delightful. "That sounds like a spectacularly fantastic way to spend the afternoon!"

"Well, it wasn't all that lovely for me," Alice says. "In fact, it was very trying."

"Have any more?" you ask.

"More what?" she asks.

"Upelkuchen cake and Downsie Drinkies," you say patiently.

AFTER ALICE takes her leave of you and your friends, you bid the others good day, stretch your legs, and head into the woods.

"Hello, hello," you greet the sweet-faced flowers.

"Hello, hello," they answer.

You spot banners flapping in the distance. Of course! It must now be the day of the Horunvendush Fair! Now *that* will be entertaining! You pick up your pace, then stop.

Your family also makes the Horunvendush Fair a major outing. Everyone will be there—including your father. You're still in no mood to see him. In fact, sitting at that table, never able to have your tea, gave you plenty of time to stew over the cruel things he said to you.

You kick a stone and it skitters into the brush. You *love* the Horunvendush Fair. You take a deep breath, then stride purposefully toward the fairgrounds. You're not going to miss it just because you had a fight with your father. Besides, your brothers and sisters and cousins will all be there, too, and you always have a good time with them.

But as you approach the festive fairgrounds, you hear

Continue on page 130.

Then you feel something tickling your knees and you suspect Mally is climbing up your leg. You hope she is bringing the Downsie potion with her. Otherwise she'll have to make another trip.

In any case, this could take a looooooooooooooong time. Well, at least the view from up here is spectacular!

THE END

BEING SO LARGE IS RATHER INCONVENIENT,
ESPECIALLY AS MOST OF YOUR HATS
ARE QUITE A BIT SMALLER THAN THE
CURRENT SIZE OF YOUR HEAD. TO SHRINK
DOWN AND TRY ANOTHER PATH, GO
BACK TO PAGE 2 AND START AGAIN.

shrieks and screams—and they are *not* of delight. You stumble backward at the terrifying sight of the Jabberwocky, that dreadful dragon, beating its enormous wings as it lands on top of a small hill at the edge of the fair. It lets out a piercing howl, then breathes out searing flames. Everything nearby is instantly scorched.

"No!" you cry. You have to find your family! You push against the panicking crowds racing in all directions and frantically scan the area. A row of colorful stalls goes up in flames as the Jabberwocky blasts another section of the fair. You can feel the heat on your cheeks, but you press on.

A woman screams as her horse runs away with her. You quickly grab the reins. Only as you calm the horse and lead it to safety do you realize who the rider is: Princess Mirana! She calls her thanks after you as you race back to the fairgrounds.

But it is now a devastated wasteland. You stand staring at the smoking remains of your father's favorite hat as it comes to a slow stop at your feet.

Your heart sinks to the pit of your stomach. They must all be dead. Victims of the Jabberwocky attack.

You don't know if you can bear it. Your last words to your father were said in anger. The last words you ever heard from him were that he was disappointed in you. And the rest of your family—perhaps you could have saved them if you had all been together.

What should you do now?

SEEK REVENGE AGAINST THE JABBERWOCKY
BY TURNING TO PAGE 133 AND FLIPPING
THE BOOK?

OR WOULD IT BE BETTER JUST TO TRY TO
MOVE ON WITH YOUR LIFE? TURN TO PAGE 134.

A searing burst of flame ignites a bush beside you. The Jabberwocky is in pursuit!

With each roar of the Jabberwocky, your heart pounds so hard you can practically see it bouncing in your chest. You don't dare look back; it could sear your eyes shut!

The Jabberwocky crashes through the brush, setting bits of the forest on fire! Flames lick at your heels, heat from its fiery breath making sweat pour down your back. Is this the end of you? Are you going to burn up in an inferno?

Then you see it: your way out! A lake!

You fling yourself into the water and swim as fast as you can. The Jabberwocky sends out a shooting blast of fire after you, but it is immediately extinguished. The creature paces back and forth on the shore, roaring and howling in frustration.

You swim to the opposite shore. You have no idea where you are, but you know that you are dripping wet.

You trudge for a day or two until you arrive at a town. "Excuse me," you say to a colorfully dressed passerby. "Where am I?"

She looks puzzled. "Why, you're here, of course."

"Ah. But where is here, exactly?"

"Where we're standing," she replies.

"But what if I were standing over there?" You point across the street.

"Then you'd be there. But it could be here. If you went there." She gives you a suspicious look. "Say, are you putting

Continue on page 135.

YOU SPEND days in Tulgey Woods trying to track the Jabberwocky. You follow clues like scorched tree stumps and smoking moss. Exhausted, you rest under a Tumtum tree, trying to figure out where to look next.

There's a sudden cracking of tree branches. Your stomach twists when you hear the whiffling sounds. The burbling. The Jabberwocky is approaching!

You slip around to the other side of the Tumtum tree to get up your courage. "As soon as I see its flaming eyes," you tell yourself, "I'll whip out my Vorpal sword and go snicker-snack!"

Hang on.

You haven't got the Vorpal sword.

You were so intent on vengeance that you forgot a crucial detail: legend has it that the Jabberwocky can be defeated only with the Vorpal sword.

And you very definitely do not have that. In fact, you've never even seen it.

"Retreat!" you cry. You dash through the woods.

YOU DECIDE that the best tribute to your family is to have a good life making good hats. You push down the sadness as the years pass.

Then, one day, you and Bayard are in the woods having a delightful game of fetch. He throws sticks farther and farther each time. You scramble after one on all fours and find yourself back at the site of the Horunvendush Fair. Even all these years later, the ground still smokes from the Jabberwocky's flaming attack. You don't like being here, but you're determined to bring back the stick. You're snuffling around an old tree stump when a flash of blue catches your eye.

Puzzled, you reach into the stump and find a little blue hat. Your mouth drops open. This is the very same paper hat you gave your father when you were just a little hatter. He must have kept it! And this is where the Jabberwocky attack took place all those years ago. Your father must have left the little blue hat for you here as a sign that your family survived. Your mouth snaps shut when it dawns on you what this means: your parents, your siblings, your aunt, your uncle, your cousins—they're *alive*!

Continue on page 136.

me on?" Then she glances around and grins. "Did my sister tell you to ask these silly questions? She's always pulling pranks."

You like the sound of a sister who plays pranks—and this delightfully daffy girl, for that matter. They seem like your kind of people. You clap her on the shoulder. "I think we're all going to get along fine."

You stay here and go into business making flame-retardant hats, to help protect the citizens from the Jabberwocky. Not only are they spectacularly silly; they are decidedly practical.

You think your father would have been proud of you in

THE END.

NOW THAT YOU'VE DONE YOUR BEST TO
HELP FLAME-PROOF THE CITIZENS, PERHAPS
SOME OTHER FRIENDS OF YOURS COULD USE
YOUR ASSISTANCE. TURN BACK TO PAGE 2
TO SEE WHO ELSE YOU CAN HELP—OR BE.

You leap about, then go into your Frabjous Dance of Joy. You run to Bayard and tell him you've got some exciting news. You're going to tell him and all your friends as soon as you both get home. It's more fun that way.

But when you share your discovery, you're shocked! Nobody believes you. Not a single, solitary one of your friends thinks that your family is still alive. They try to convince you that you're wrong, but you refuse to listen to them.

There's so much to do! You must prepare for your family's return. You change your appearance and concentrate on work. You become the serious fellow your father hoped you'd be.

But there's something you don't understand. If they're alive, why have they not come home? Is your father *that* disappointed in you? So disappointed that he never wanted to see you again?

This saddens you so much you take to your bed.

Then, one day, Alice bursts in and announces she has proof that your family is still alive—and being held captive by the Red Queen. You rally, your energy returning. You are determined to fight to bring them home!

And perhaps the best news of all? Your friends are in this fight with you!

⌇⌇

"This is the only way to travel," you tell Alice as you kneel beside her on the Bandersnatch's back. It easily galumphs across the miles of harsh terrain, peaks, and glaciers on the way to the Red

Queen's stronghold in the Outlands. Behind you, Mirana and McTwisp are astride the queen's white horse, and Mally rides atop Bayard. A horsedrawn cart carrying the Tweedles follows. You turn and gesture madly, urging your friends to keep up.

In the distance, you see a large heart-shaped fortress that seems to be entirely made of bloodred roots, branches, vines, and leaves. Alice signals to stop at the top of a hill to strategize.

"My family is there!" you declare. "I know it!"

"And if they are, we'll rescue them," Alice promises.

Mallmykun suggests that the group split up to gain more ground.

You and Alice climb down from the Bandersnatch. "We'll have to go by foot from here. Don't want to attract attention. At least," you add with a gleeful smirk, "not yet."

You can hardly wait until you are reunited with your family! What a celebration you'll have!

But when you and Alice sneak into the Red Queen's private chambers, the root-, plant-, and leaf-infested room is empty. No family!

SHOULD YOU SEARCH ELSEWHERE?
GO TO PAGE 139 AND FLIP THE BOOK.

OR DO YOU WANT TO TAKE
ONE LAST LOOK AROUND? TURN TO PAGE 142.

with the head, talons, and wings of an eagle attached to the body of a lion bounds toward you. Following more slowly is a large Turtle.

"Excuse me, dear Gryphon," you say, tipping your hat to the creature. "I'm looking for my family."

"No time for that now!" the Gryphon informs you as the Turtle nudges you toward shore. "The dance is about to begin! You can look for them when you change partners."

"What are we dancing?" you ask, scanning the assortment of people, animals, and things in-between joining hands in groups.

"The Lobster Quadrille, of course!" the Turtle says.

You've heard of this lively number but never seen it performed, as it requires not only a large body of water but a vast quantity of lobsters. You see that both are in abundance here.

"Will you, won't you, will you, won't you, won't you join the dance?" the crowd sings.

As a lobster grips your hand in its claw, you realize you don't exactly have a choice.

Continue on page 141.

"**I** GUESS we'll have to keep looking," you tell Alice. You leave Iracebeth's private chambers and rejoin your friends. None of them have located your family, either.

"We'll have to broaden our search," Alice suggests. "Maybe Iracebeth was afraid they'd be too easy to find in her castle."

"We'll split up again," Bayard suggests, "but cast a wider net."

A plan in place, you all go your separate ways.

You make your way to the Tear-full Lake. Underland legend says it got its name because it was made by the tears cried by a giant. You're not sure if that's true, but you decide to keep an eye out for overlarge beings. Think of the hatting possibilities!

You spot a crowd assembling at the shore. Perhaps your family is among them! You hurry toward them. A creature the castle all along. Now your new mission is to find some dry clothes.

⌒⌒⌒

THE END

RETURN TO PAGE 2 TO TRY A NEW
PATH, PREFERABLY A DRIER ONE.

The dance is rather complicated. Several lines face each other, and everyone has a lobster as a partner on each side. The Turtle and the Gryphon keep time as seals, sea urchins, and oysters sing from the rocks. The lines dance toward each other, then dance away.

"Somersaults!" the Gryphon cries.

You flip over and over, along with your fellow dancers. As the world goes topsy-turvy, you scan the lines for Hightopps. So far, no sign of them, but there are many, many dancers.

"Now throw as hard as you can!" the Turtle shouts.

All the dancers shriek as they run toward the water. You run with them, clutching your lobster partner's claw.

"Hang on," you huff as you dash to the shoreline. "Who throws whom?"

The Lobster gives you a mischievous grin. Suddenly, you are flung into the water.

You splash around, trying to get right side up. You burst to the surface to see your lobster partner giggling onshore. You look around and see you're the only non-lobster in the lake. All the lobsters bob and laugh around you.

You start swimming back to shore. It may take a while with the lobsters tugging you under, grabbing at your nose with their claws, and otherwise making themselves nuisances.

But when you do make it to the beach, you're greeted with a happy surprise: your family has been found! They were in

YOU JUST can't accept that your family isn't here in this forest-gone-mad room. You were so sure they were here! You could feel it.

You scan the rotting vegetables, scattered leaves, and bizarre contraptions you don't even want to identify in the Red Queen's odd organic fortress. Your eyes land on a curious freestanding gold frame. You pick it up and realize that it's actually a very ornate ant farm. Then your eyes widen. A hat is being sketched in the sand!

You bring the ant farm close to your face. It can't be! But it is!

You smile through your tears as you realize what you're looking at: tiny people. They gesture wildly and seem to be shouting, but they're so little you can't hear anything.

"Father! Mother! Everyone!" you cry. "It's you! Teeny, tiny yous!" You kiss the glass pane and then giggle as your family tumbles about in the sand.

Alice comes to stand beside you. "You found them!" she says.

You nod at her, beaming with joy.

And then, suddenly, gates crash down over the windows. You turn to see the bloody Big Head herself standing in the doorway. She's smiling in an especially sinister fashion.

This can't be good.

Alice is grabbed by two vegetable guards and Iracebeth yanks a peculiar device from Alice's pocket.

"Thank you ever so much!" Iracebeth gloats. "You have delivered to me the most powerful device in the entire Universe."

The expression on Alice's face tells you that this is not a welcome turn of events. Things aren't improved when more vegetable footmen drag in all your friends. Prisoners, the lot of you. "I recall now why I don't like her," you mutter.

"Now we shall see justice," Iracebeth trumpets, then strides out of the room. The other prisoners are dragged out with her. A gate drops, trapping you and Alice inside.

You pick up the ant farm. Your father cups his hands around his mouth.

"Tarrant?" he calls in his tiny voice. "Is that really you? I'd stopped believing so long ago, it feels impossible."

"It's not impossible, merely *un*possible." You fiddle in your pocket and pull out the little blue hat to show him. His smile covers his tiny face.

"Oh, Hatter," Alice cries, trying unsuccessfully to squeeze through the gate. "What have I done? We have to stop her! We have to get out of here!"

You look at Alice, then at the paper hat, then at your family inside the ant farm. "I think I have an idea."

❧

After some quick adjustments, conversations, and descriptions, you stand at the barred window, holding a blue paper airplane made from your little hat. Your father sits inside it in the pilot's position. He's carefully checking how sturdy the thing is.

"I feel like I've traded the frying pan for the fire," he shouts up at you. "This is crazy."

"Someone once said wisdom is born from total insanity," you tell him.

His face twists in confusion. "Who said that?"

"Me, just now," you reply.

You lift the airplane holding your father up to the window. You experiment with several angles to find the perfect launching position.

"Ready?" you ask, but you don't wait for an answer. You hurl the paper airplane through the bars. You're pretty sure the tinny little sound you hear is your father yelling as he takes to the air.

Now all you can do is wait. And hope.

❧

Very soon you hear growling, snorting, snuffling, and thwumping. Can it be . . . ?

Massive teeth chomp down on the gate, ripping it right out of the wall.

"Yes!" you cheer. "Bandersnatch to the rescue!" Your plan worked! Sending your tiny father out on the teeny airplane to find the gigantic Bandersnatch was risky, but it paid off!

"We're free!" Alice cries.

You hold up your hand and the Bandersnatch bends down. Your father jumps into your palm.

"You did it!" you congratulate him.

"It was your plan," he says proudly.

"Now to grow you back . . ." you tell him.

You scan the room and spot an elegant tea tray. A dome-covered plate looks promising. You lift the top, revealing a tiny cake with the words *Eat Me* written in icing. "Aha!" you exclaim.

You take a piece of cake. "Not too much, now!" you warn your family.

One by one, they each take a bite of cake and pass it along, quickly returning to their normal sizes. You are amused when Alice averts her eyes. Silly girl. Of course their clothes wouldn't grow with them. Your mother sets to finding things to wrap everyone in before your father approaches you slowly.

He stands in front of you. "I see you haven't changed a bit."

"Nope," you tell him. You brace yourself, wondering how he'll react.

There's a moment of silence, then . . . "Good," he says with a sharp nod.

Every bit of you smiles. Your toes curl happily, your nose perks up, your chest expands, and you feel ten feet tall—without taking a single bite of the Upelkuchen cake! Your family—alive! Reunited! And your father beaming at you with pride—a sight you feared you'd never see. Now here it is, even better than you ever dreamed it. You feel lit up inside.

You are reaching out to give him a hug when an odd thing happens. Suddenly, you're all moving in slow motion. It doesn't last very long, but you're all bewildered by the strange ripple in time.

"What the dickens was that?" your father sputters.

Patches of rust appear in the walls and floor. You hear Alice gasp.

"Time! He's slowing down," she says. "He's going to stop! It's why he wanted the Chronosphere."

"Hang on!" you say. "If Time ends, we'll *all* end. He told me so himself."

"This is my fault," Alice says. "I stole the Chronosphere! I should have listened to him."

You and your family exchange looks. You all seem to agree, but they wait for you to say it. You know Alice did what she did to try to help you. You know where the blame really lies.

"We've got to stop the Big Head!" you declare.

One problem: how are you going to do that?

Since the Red Queen was so intent on that time-travel thingie, that could mean she plans to go somewhere in time. You look around the chamber. There are pieces of that Time fellow's contraption scattered on the floor. Should you put it back together? Will that get you wherever she plans to go?

Or should you try to find Iracebeth first to see exactly what she's up to?

IF YOU SEARCH FOR THE BIG HEAD WITH ALICE,
GO TO PAGE 150.

IF YOU STAY WITH YOUR FAMILY,
GO TO PAGE 149 AND FLIP THE BOOK.

A LICE BELIEVES that Iracebeth wanted the Chronosphere to go back in time to change her past. So you'd better get Time's contraption put back together in case you have to follow her there.

Alice runs off to find Iracebeth and try to talk some sense into her—which sounds like the least sensible thing anyone could possibly try to do. But that's Alice for you. In the meantime, you and your family rebuild Time's machine.

"I think that's it," your father declares, tightening a final screw.

You and all the other Hightopps take a step back to admire your handiwork. It's a marvelously demented piece of machinery! Like a tasteful metal fascinator made for a giant's head.

"Should we bring it to Alice?" you mother asks.

You frown. "Actually, I think I'd better test it. Safety first."

You climb aboard and study the gadgets, gewgaws, levers, and buttons for a moment. You press a promising-looking button. The machine roars to life. You grin: it works!

Continue on page 151.

ALICE ASKS your family to gather up the pieces of that machine while the two of you track down Iracebeth. You rush through the castle and discover that everyone is in the palace garden. It looks as if Big Head is presiding over a trial in which she is the prosecutor, judge, and jury. Executioner, too, you realize grimly.

Alice interrupts the proceedings, but Iracebeth grabs Mirana and jumps into the whirring, twirling, glowing Chronosphere. They vanish.

Vegetable footmen approach you and Alice. You don't much like their menacing attitude. Just as they reach out for you, an enormous roar stops them in their tracks.

"Reinforcements!" you cheer. The Bandersnatch, carrying your family members, bounds into the garden.

Everyone scatters, and you and Alice take the opportunity to rush over to Time. You untie him as Alice tries to rouse him. Rust spreads over his body.

"I let my heart distract me from the schedule," Time says mournfully. "I'm a disgrace to the profession, the concept, myself."

Continue on page 152.

Too bad you can't figure out how to control it!

You pop around all over the past, the present, and even the future, never stopping long enough to get off the gollysnarking contraption! And there are no signs of it ever coming to

an

END.

THE CHRONOSPHERE FINALLY BREAKS
DOWN AFTER AN IMMEASURABLE AMOUNT
OF TIME, AND YOU FIND YOURSELF BACK
AT THE BEGINNING. TURN BACK TO PAGE
2 AND START A NEW ADVENTURE.

He may be a pretentious old fogey, but you can't help yourself: the bloke needs cheering up. "C'mon, old chap," you say. "Don't give yourself a hard time. Besides, you're the only person who can rebuild that thing!" You point at the pieces of machinery your family lays out in front of him.

"The Tempus Fugit," Time murmurs. He looks up at you and smiles.

No one can resist you when you really try, you think with more than a little pride. *Not even Time.*

———

You chortle with joy as Alice expertly guides the Tempus Whatsit across the Ocean of Time. You really wish she weren't in such a hurry: there are so many wonderful images floating by so quickly! You'd love to hop out and revisit a few.

But no. There's this whole save-all-of-time-and-the-Universe problem to deal with first. Perhaps on the way back . . .

Iracebeth has brought Mirana back to when they were little girls. You don't understand why—until Mirana makes a confession. All those years ago, Mirana told a lie and betrayed her sister . . . and that one lie has stayed with the Iracebeth ever since.

You're shocked! Mirana has always seemed like a paragon of everything good. And Iracebeth, well, not so much. But here is the White Queen herself admitting that much of what went so horribly wrong for Iracebeth was *Mirana's* fault. Just as Iracebeth has been claiming all these years.

Go figure.

Then you see a sight that makes you clutch your heart. You don't know if you can take any more surprises. Iracebeth and Mirana—both crying—are now hugging! And—gasp—*smiling*!

Then something truly bizarre happens. A door flings open. Standing in the doorway is a little girl—a little girl who looks surprisingly like Iracebeth only with an ordinarily sized head.

Her eyes travel up to the Red Queen's enormous head and heart-shaped do, and she lets out a shriek.

Who can blame her, really . . .

Poof! The little girl and the Big Head suddenly turn into rust-covered statues. And the minute they do, rust begins spreading everywhere.

"Oh, this can't be good," you mutter.

"She has broken the past!" Time cries. "We have to get to the Grand Clock before it stops forever!"

So everyone gets into the whirligig thingamabob—the, uh, Chronosphere!

Good thing you don't get airsick. You have a feeling this is going to be a wild ride!

⁕

You cling to anything you can get your fingers curled around as Alice navigates the Chronosphere across the Ocean of Time. You nervously peer over your shoulder. Enormous rust waves crash behind you. Everything they roll over freezes and turns to rust.

Just like her, you think, scowling at the Red Queen, now a rust-covered statue cradled in Mirana's lap. This is all her fault. Even frozen Big Head causes trouble.

"I still don't see why we had to bring her," you mutter. Mirana and Iracebeth may have made up, but that doesn't mean you have to like Iracebeth.

You look around. Below you, rust is spreading across the land, freezing grass, trees, buildings, and people! Even the snowflakes pause mid-air and are turned a muddy red.

And behind you, the days stop. The waves are gaining on you. This isn't looking good.

"I've really enjoyed our time together," you tell Alice, trying to keep a brave face.

She expertly zooms into Time's castle, even as the walls turn to rust and crumble.

Maybe it's not over yet. . . .

Crash!

The Chronosphere smashes through a window and crashes to the floor in the Chamber of the Grand Clock. You, Alice, Time, Mirana, and Iracebeth tumble out.

The Chronosphere snaps back to its small size. Alice grabs it and runs. You follow close behind, dodging and weaving through the deluge of rust.

You pass rusted mechanical men lying about the floor. "We did our best, sir," one of them gasps, then collapses.

Alice keeps going, and you run after her. Rust flows in from all sides. You turn and see that the rust has completely enveloped Time. He collapses to the floor.

"Alice!" you call.

But she doesn't stop running and rushes into the giant clock, rust nearly upon her. You stand frozen and stare down at the rust creeping up your legs as she slams the Chronosphere into place.

But did she save Time in time?

Everything goes deadly quiet.

And then you hear a wonderful sound. A beautiful sound. A frabjous sound! A *tick*. And then a *tock*! Then a *ticktock ticktock ticktock*.

Time is resuming! The rust is receding!

She did it!

Before you can congratulate Alice, you hear your father call your name. You turn to see your unrusted family coming into the room. You rush to embrace them, each and every one.

You grip your father's arm. "Father! This whole time I thought you were . . . but you weren't! And you couldn't come see me because you were . . . and you kept the hat!"

"Of course I kept it," Zanik says. "It was a gift from you. But the greatest gift we have is the time we have together, and I promise I'll never waste another second."

You beam.

"We have a lot of catching up to do," Zanik says.

You decide there's no time like the present. "I make hats,

Father!" you say proudly. "I'm a hatter, just like you."

Zanik's eyes tear up. "I want to see every one, Tarrant. I want to see every hat you've ever made."

You dash over to Alice and grab her hand. "Come, Alice, you must meet my family. You'll love them. We're all going to have so much fun together."

But Alice hesitates. You frown, wondering what's wrong. Then it dawns on you. "Oh, but I'm forgetting you have a family of your own, don't you?" you say.

She nods. You eye Mirana and Iracebeth, the Tweedle brothers, your parents, your aunts, your uncles, and your cousins. "Very important thing, a family," you say. "You only get the one."

"Hatter, I think it's time for me to go home," Alice says.

You smile, letting her know you understand.

You bid Alice au revoir—until you meet again. You know you will someday. It's Alice, after all. Then you rejoin your family, relishing this reunion.

You and your father go into business together, making twice as many hats as ever. And you and your family live happily ever after. Now that's what you'd call a frabjous

END.

YOU'VE GOTTEN YOUR VERY OWN FAMILY BACK.
WELL DONE! NOW IT IS TIME TO TURN BACK
TO PAGE 2 AND TRY BEING SOMEONE ELSE.

THE RED QUEEN

YOU PUT the finishing touches on your makeup and then go meet Time for your date. You slip inside the grandfather clock you use to get to Time's castle. It's a little hard to fit your generously sized head into the clock, but you manage.

You enter his grand parlor and hold out your hand. Time kisses it, tickling you with his mighty mustache as he does.

"Oh, my radiant and beautiful dial-face, bulbous of head and soft of heart," he says, standing back upright. "You are my only beacon. Here: a gift—nay, a tribute!"

He holds out a small music box. Your face lights up. You do love presents!

"How sweet!" you say, taking the box. "Dear old tick-tock!"

He blushes when he hears your nickname for him. "I-I know how you love tiny things," he stammers.

You open the box. A delicate melody plays. The box top shows a mechanized miniature tableau of an executioner and a king with his head on the block. The ax falls and the king's head drops into a basket. The head then reattaches, and the ax repositions as the melody ends. How adorable! You giggle girlishly.

"I'll treasure it forever," you say. Then you toss it onto the sofa and sigh. Murderous miniatures are all very well and good, but what you really want is Time's Chronosphere.

Time frowns. "Something troubling you, my dear?"

You take his hand and bat your eyelashes at him. "You know what I desire! With my big brain and your little Chronosphere, we could together rule the past, the present, and the future!"

Time's face falls. "But my dear Iracebeth, I've told you time and again that's out of the question. You ask the impossible. You cannot change the past."

You turn away from him, rage bubbling inside you. You need that Chronosphere. It's the only way to show all those rotten, vile people who so mistreated you that they can't push you around.

Time gestures to his cabinet of magic beans, dodo birds, trinkets, and other odds and ends. "My dear, I would happily part with any one of my diversions! But I cannot give you the Chronosphere!"

Is this possible? Is he actually refusing you? *Again? You?* You're appalled! You figured he would've come around by now. There's really only so many times you can be refused before heads must roll. Although, a headless Time wouldn't be any good to you.

Hmmm. How do you want to play this?

YOU CAN SHOUT LOUDER.
THAT USUALLY GETS YOU WHAT YOU WANT.
GO TO PAGE 163 AND FLIP THE BOOK.

POUTING SOMETIMES WORKED
WHEN YOU WERE A LITTLE GIRL.
TO TRY THAT, TURN TO PAGE 164.

TIME IS being ridiculous. All this nonsense about how time travel has severe consequences, how if your past self sees your future self, dire things will happen, blah blah blah. No, you are getting that Chronsophere and you are getting it now. With a shouting match.

Usually when you shout, the person you're shouting at gives in. You can outshout pretty much everyone.

But not Time. He shouts the same infuriating statement over and over back at you: "Sorry, but I can't!"

You shout louder and louder and louder, until finally you take in a deep breath and let out the loudest shout ever—so loud you break the sound barrier!

Unfortunately, it shatters the castle, the Chronosphere, and all of Underland.

Oops. That wasn't how you hoped this would

END.

Continue on page 165.

"**YOU WOULD** if you loved me!" You let your lower lip quiver. Then you stick it out in a serious pout.

"But I do love you—" Time begins. Suddenly, a shiver goes through his body. A strange look comes over his face. He glances down toward his chest.

"The Grand Clock!" he gasps. He charges out of the room.

"Huh?" You stare at the spot where he was standing. What just happened? Did he actually run away from your best pout of all time?

You run after him, dashing into the Chamber of the Grand Clock. Time has sunk to his knees. You shriek when you see none other than that dastardly Alice disappear—in *your* Chronosphere. What the rutabaga is *she* doing here?

Time points a shaking finger at the Grand Clock. "My Chronosphere. She got it after all!"

"Alice? *The* Alice?" You feel your face growing purple with rage.

Continue on page 166.

WELL, SINCE YOU'VE ALREADY DESTROYED
EVERYTHING, YOU MIGHT AS WELL TRAVEL
BACK TO PAGE 2 AND TRY A DIFFERENT
PATH. THE CONSEQUENCES OF TIME
TRAVEL CAN'T BE WORSE THAN THIS!

BACK TO PAGE 2

Time cowers as you stomp closer to him. "The White Queen's champion who defeated the Jabberwocky? The very reason I have been banished from my kingdom? She was here—and you didn't think to tell me?" You are vibrating with fury.

"I-I-I didn't realize!" Time stammers.

You bring your face close to his. "Idiot!" you cry into his ashen face. "Imbecile! You let Alice *steal the Chronosphere*?"

"It's happening already!" he says, looking dazed. "Without the Chronosphere the Great Clock will unwind. Time myself will stop!"

This is too much.

SHOULD YOU JUST SHOUT
"OFF WITH HIS HEAD!" AND BE DONE WITH IT?
GO TO PAGE 169 AND FLIP THE BOOK.

OR DO YOU GIVE HIM ONE CHANCE
TO MAKE THIS RIGHT? GO TO PAGE 167.

IT TAKES every ounce of strength you have not to throttle him. But you have a better idea.

"I'm feeling very generous because I like my little music box," you tell him through clenched teeth. "I am giving you one last chance. You will find a way to get back that Chronosphere. Then you will give it to me!"

Time appears to be dazed. Has he even heard one word you've said?

"Wilkins, get in here!" Time cries. "We've got a Tempus Fugit to build."

What did he say? A Temper Futsit? No matter. As long as it's something that will bring back the Chronosphere, you don't care about the details. At least he's on top of it. You return to your castle in the Outlands to wait.

And wait.

And wait some more.

This is boring.

Nothing exciting happens when you live in an organic castle in the middle of nowhere. Especially when your servants are vegetables. What to do, what to do. . . .

Continue on page 168.

GO OUT TO YOUR ORGANIC COURTYARD BY
TURNING TO PAGE 171 AND FLIPPING THE BOOK.
PERHAPS SOMETHING WILL AMUSE YOU
OUT THERE.

GO LOOK AT YOUR ANT FARM BY TURNING TO
PAGE 172. THAT OFTEN RESTORES YOUR MOOD.

YOU RESORT to your usual method of solving problems. *"Off with his head!"* you shout at the top of your lungs.

Your guards rush into the room and arrest Time.

Only thing is, when Time is, er, *arrested*, everything stops, bringing the whole world—including *you*—to a standstill.

Unfortunately, frozen like this, you can't exactly tell the guards to let Time go. Besides, you really don't like reversing your queenly orders. So everything stays like this forever and ever. Without

END.

THE ONLY WAY TO START MOVING AND
SHOUTING AGAIN IS TO TURN TO PAGE 2
AND TAKE A DIFFERENT PATH.

As the vegetable man is dragged off, you mutter, "How many times must we go through this?"

You turn your back on the offending shrubbery and go back inside your organic castle. You walk along the root-infested corridors, smiling at the vegetables on spikes along the walls. You stop when you spot a misty figure approaching.

"Why don't you curtsy?" you demand. She must be one of your courtiers, given how fancy her dress is. She has a refreshingly large head. But she just stares at you, an unpleasant expression on her face.

"What are you looking at?" You pat your hair, in case she has noticed some strands out of place. Infuriating! She does the same thing.

"Stop that!" you shout, pointing at her.

She points back at you.

She's mimicking your every move and gesture! That dreadful Knave of Hearts used to torment you the same way when you were children. You stamp your foot indignantly. So does she!

"That's it! Off with her head!" you bellow, pointing at her. She points back. She should be looking much more afraid. This makes you even angrier.

"*Off with her head!*" you shout over and over.

Two vegetable guards appear by your sides. "Are you sure?" one of them asks nervously.

"Imbecile!" you shriek. "Do you want to lose your head, too?"

Continue on page 173.

YOU STROLL through your red, vine-covered court-yard, trailed, as always, by your vegetable footmen. You notice some of your other vegetable servants carrying cans of red paint and hurrying toward a particularly suspicious-looking section of the courtyard. "What is going on?" you demand.

One of the veggie-men whips his paint can around his back and bows. "Good afternoon, Your Majesty."

"Don't give me that. Tell me what you're doing!"

The vegetable servants exchange nervous looks. "We, er, that is . . ." one begins.

"Off with his head!" you bellow. "For not getting to the point!"

"Some of the plants have sprouted white buds. We know how much Your Highness detests the color, so we're painting over them," another footman blurts as the one who took too long is hauled away.

Your eyes widen, then narrow. "Well, thank you for telling the truth." You point at him. "Off with his head for telling me a truth I don't like!"

YOU ENTER your private chambers and go to the ant farm sitting on your bedside table. You peer through the glass panes at the tiny village sitting on top of an elaborate network of tunnels.

Only there aren't any ants inside. They're tiny little people—people *you* captured, shrunk, and put there.

"You should have known better than to make me look foolish." You sneer at the miniaturized Hightopps staring at you from their ant farm prison. "It may take a while, but I *always* get my revenge."

You stride around the room, gloating. "It was a brilliant plan," you brag. You enjoy this, even though you've gone over the details of your revenge dozens of time. It must be the captive audience.

"You were so easy to fool, drinking up the shrinking potion. You wriggled so much in that sack that Stayne nearly dropped you. Oh, but then!" You clap your hands. "Oh, the glorious terror I unleashed when I let the Jabberwocky loose at the Horunvendush Fair! The screams! The panic!"

Continue on page 174.

"If you insist, Your Majesty." Suddenly, you're surrounded by ten guards. So is your nemesis.

Your *reflected* nemesis.

You caught sight of yourself in a large but unwashed mirror.

So there goes your head. Because you always get what you ask for in

᠆ᢀᢁ᠆

THE END.

ER; YOU MIGHT NEED TO TRY SOMEONE
ELSE'S HEAD NOW THAT YOU'VE LOST
YOURS. GO BACK TO PAGE 2.

You bring your face right up to the pane of glass. "And the despair your ridiculous son felt ever after." You flick the glass with a finger. "That'll teach him to laugh at me."

You turn to a tea tray with a dome-covered plate. You lift it to reveal a tiny cake. *EAT ME* is written across the top in frosting.

"So close and yet so far," you chortle as you replace the lid. "Hey, I'm talking to you!" You tap the glass to annoy them. Then you pick it up and shake it. "Earthquake! Ha-ha!"

Hearing a distant noise, you stop abruptly. You cross to a nearby window and yank back the curtain. Up in the sky, Time careens straight toward you on an extraordinary contraption. You jump back just as Time flies through the window and crashes to the floor.

The contraption breaks into a hundred pieces. Time lies flushed, sweating, and gasping at your feet.

"Where the devil have you been?" you demand. "Where is Alice? Where's my Chronosphere?"

"She's gone!" Time huffs. "She took it!"

"What? You let her get away?" you shriek.

This day is not going at all the way you thought it would!

Time stands unsteadily. He pulls back his cloak and points to his heart clock, which is ticking ever more slowly and softly. Rust now covers most of the clock face.

"You don't understand!" Time pleads. "I must find her! Where is she?"

You fling up your hands. "How should I know where she is?"

"She's your enemy. She—" He stops, remembering something. "Hightopps! She kept talking about Hightopps! She says she knows where they are! She said she was going to rescue them. Do you know what that means?"

You turn away, thinking. Your eyes flick to the ant farm. A plan forms in your mind. A wicked grin spreads across your face.

"I know exactly what it means," you say. You poke your head out the door and call, "Guards!"

A pair of giant vegetable footmen enter. You tip your head toward Time. "Put him in the dungeon!" you order.

"What? Wait! My dearest, you can't!" Time protests. "It will not work. It is impossible to stop Time!"

The footmen grab Time and hold him tight.

"Oh, it *is* possible," Time murmurs. "Who knew?"

You stand in front of him, your arms crossed. "From now on, I'm in charge! Take him away!"

You watch as the footmen drag the crestfallen man out

of the room. It is really too bad. You and tick-tock could have been Underland's most powerful couple. But he's just another disappointment.

You go to the window. It will only be a matter of time before Alice and her infernal friends arrive as part of their blasted mission—which, come to think of it, might not be such a bad thing. Hmmm . . . yes. This might all work out perfectly.

⁓

It's all coming together splendidly. All that's left is to lure that awful Alice into your trap. And you are positive your bait will be irresistible. Plus it will continue to punish the terrible Hightopps at the same time.

You peer through a keyhole into the corridor. Your plan is working! Alice and the Hatter race past you. They're falling for your trap!

You burst into the hallway. "Now!" you shout. You dance with glee as gates fall over the windows of your private chambers. You step into the doorway, backed up by your imposing vegetable footmen.

"Hello, Alice!" you say. Oh, you just love it when you make those horrified expressions appear on the faces of your enemies. And those expressions are now on the faces of Alice and the Hatter. You snap your fingers and two footmen step forward and seize Alice.

"Thank you ever so much!" you tell her sweetly. You yank the Chronosphere roughly from her pocket. You hold it up so it catches the light. "You have delivered to me the most powerful device in the entire Universe."

You cock your head, listening. Yes, those are the footsteps you've been waiting for. You smile. "Along with the person whom I hold truly responsible."

You turn to see a delicious sight: footmen escort your sister, Mirana, the White Queen, who stole your crown from you not just once but *twice*! You frown when you see that she is maintaining her composure. Well, you'll take care of that soon enough.

❧

You twirl your judge's gavel, ready to preside over the court you've set up in the castle garden. Mirana—the accused—stands in the center. The White Rabbit, McTwisp, stands next to her as her advocate. Her coconspirators are held prisoner by your giant vegetable footmen. That meddlesome Alice and the irritating Hatter are still locked up inside your castle.

You preen in front of your garden throne. Time slumps, bound with chains, on the king's throne, clutching his heart, which barely ticks at all.

You point your finger at the accused. "Mirana of Marmoreal!" you declare. "You are accused of treason! I hereby sentence you to—"

The White Rabbit jumps up, interrupting you. "Wait! What about the verdict?"

"Sentence first!" you snap. "Then verdict!"

You turn back to Mirana. You will now condemn her to the same punishment you have suffered. "You are banished to the Outlands," you declare, your voice trembling with emotion. "No one is to show you kindness or ever speak a word to you. You will not have a friend in the world."

Mirana looks bewildered. "What are the charges against me?"

You can't believe it! How can she pretend to be so innocent? It is outrageous! "You have lied. You have stolen. You are *not* the rightful queen of Underland!"

The rabbit, McTwisp, interrupts again. "Objection! Where's your proof?"

You spin around to face him. "I don't need proof!" you exclaim triumphantly. "I've got better!" You lift the Chronosphere. "I shall have a confession!"

You glare at Mirana. She shrinks back, unsettled. Good. It's about time some cracks appeared in that oh-so-perfect facade of hers. And once you have that confession from her, everyone will see that their perfect princess is nothing but a lying cheat! And you will be restored to your rightful place.

You throw the Chronosphere to the ground. It pops to full size, glowing, ready for travel.

"Wait!" someone cries. "Stop! Wait!"

"Another interruption?" you snarl. You whirl around. Unbelievable. It's *Alice*, causing you trouble once again!

"You cannot change the past, Your Majesty," she says very seriously. "Believe me, I have tried."

SHOULD YOU CONTINUE TO INTERROGATE MIRANA?
SHE'LL CRACK AND CONFESS EVENTUALLY.
GO TO PAGE 181 AND FLIP THE BOOK.

OR SHOULD YOU USE THE CHRONOSPHERE TO
GO BACK IN TIME TO PROVE ONCE AND FOR
ALL THAT SHE IS GUILTY? TURN TO PAGE 184.

"FINE, FINE, fine!" you mutter. It's too much bother to go all the way back in time. Besides, there are some things you don't want to relive! With you as prosecutor, judge, and jury, you have no doubt of the outcome.

You point your gavel at Mirana. "Where were you on that fateful night?"

"Which night?" Mirana asks.

"Aha! You admit there was more than one night?"

Perplexed, Mirana looks at you. "Why, there are many nights. Just as there are many days. At least three hundred, I believe."

"You know what night we're talking about. The fragickigglick night you committed your crimes!"

"Objection!" McTwisp interjects. "That is not a word."

You whirl around and glare at the insufferable rabbit. "Of course it's a word. I just said it, didn't I? What else would I say but a word?"

"Do you mean what you say?" McTwisp asks. "And do you say what you mean?"

"They're the same thing."

Continue on page 183.

This is too much! "We're off the topic! We have to get back to—"

This time it's Alice who interrupts you. "I have a question about . . ."

You're so frustrated your head swells and swells until . . .

Oh, no! Your head *bursts*!

Well, that's quite an explosive

END!

IT SEEMS YOU'LL HAVE TO GO BACK TO PAGE 2
AND START OVER IN ORDER TO HAVE A HEAD
AGAIN. PERHAPS THIS TIME YOU SHOULD
PICK ONE THAT DOESN'T GROW SO BIG.

"Oh, no, they're not. A very common misunderstanding. But that would be like saying 'I eat what I like' and 'I like what I eat' mean the same thing."

"I don't like it when people are mean," the little Dormouse murmurs.

Oooh! They're driving you mad. "Let's get on with it!" you say. "Back to the night at hand."

The March Hare stands and points at you. "I don't see a knight in her hand. But I have one!" He holds up a chess piece.

Now the insufferable Hatter gets up and paces in front of you. He puts on a pair of spectacles and pretends to stick his thumbs in his nonexistent suspenders. "I have a few questions. How much wood would a woodchuck chuck if a woodchuck could chuck wood?"

"Hey! Who says I can't?" a voice calls out.

Unbelievable. "What's a woodchuck doing in here? Off with its head!" you screech.

The woodchuck hangs its head. "All right, it's true, I can't actually chuck wood. *Chew* it but not chuck it. So sorry. Please proceed."

"I have another question," the Hatter says. "If Peter Piper picked a peck of pickled peppers, how many pickled peppers did Peter Piper pick?"

A young gentleman stands. "I object. Is someone accusing me of unlawful picking of peppers?"

YOU SQUINCH your nose at Alice. She can't tell you what to do! You grab Mirana and yank her inside the Chronosphere. You will go back in time to the day when everything went wrong—the day your own sister betrayed you by eating all of the tarts and telling your mother it was *you*. You'll make them all see the truth!

You fly back, back, back in time. You pass over Horunvendush Day quickly, flying by the fiery scene. You don't want Mirana to know about your role in the Jabberwocky attack. You're soon hovering over Toomalie Day, but you keep going. You don't ever want to relive the humiliation of your tiara breaking in front of all of Witzend.

You grind your teeth and glare at Mirana, remembering your father pronouncing her the heir instead of you. She shrinks away from you. Good. She *should* be scared.

On and on you go. But as the days play out below you, you become intrigued.

Maybe you should stop and visit a day.

IF YOU WANT TO STOP OFF FOR A VISIT,
GO TO PAGE 187 AND FLIP THE BOOK.

IF YOU WANT TO GO STRAIGHT TO YOUR
INTENDED DESTINATION, TURN TO PAGE 188.

you. "Here," she says. "I need to get dressed for our croquet match!" As you struggle with the baby, she flounces out of the overheated kitchen.

"Stay still!" you order the baby. Then you realize what you're holding in your arms isn't a baby at all! It's a pig! You drop it to the ground just as the cook throws more pepper into the pot.

"*Ah-choo! Ah-choo! Ah-choo!*" You sneeze a hundred times more. Once you've regained control, you say, "Give me your handkerchief, Mirana."

No answer.

"Mirana?" Now that the pepper has cleared, you realize Mirana is no longer in the kitchen!

You race out the door just in time to see her take off in the Chronosphere.

Oh, no! Now you'll never be able to get back to your own time! Or any other time, for that matter!

Maybe this isn't so bad, you think as you head back into the kitchen to wait for the Duchess. *I can plot my revenge in advance, before any of the bad things actually happen. I'll show that Alice she can't get the best of me.*

Continue on page 189.

YOU CIRCLE around the images from the past until you spot one you think you'd enjoy visiting. You haven't seen the Duchess in quite a while. At one time you were very good friends.

"Just a quick hello," you tell Mirana. You lean in and snarl, "Then we'll get on to the matter of your confession!"

You jump out of the Chronosphere, dragging Mirana behind you. As you approach the Duchess's house, you hear banging, clashing, and shouting. "She must be cooking," you say. You just hope she isn't baking tarts.

You enter and instantly sneeze. "Pepper," you choke out. "Too much pepper!"

A dishpan whirls by your head.

"Don't criticize the cook," the Duchess scolds. She shifts the grunting baby she's cradling in her arms. Then her fore-head furrows. "Iracebeth, didn't you just leave? We're to play croquet any moment now." She steps toward you and looks at you and Mirana. "And why do you both look so old?"

More pots clang and crash, and the baby wriggles so much the Duchess nearly drops him. She holds him out to

YOU'RE GOING to keep going backward, to a time when *you* were the injured party!

You bring them to the destination you had in mind all along: the time when Mirana lied about the tart crusts. The day that set all this in motion! The day she ruined your life!

"Here we are," you say. You are back at Witzend Castle on a snowy night—the night that changed Underland forever.

The Chronosphere alights in a corridor. You see patches of rust spreading throughout the castle, but you don't have time to yell at anyone about it right now. You yank Mirana out, and the Chronosphere shrinks.

"Where are we?" she asks.

"You know where we are," you tell her.

You step over the Chronosphere and pull a reluctant Mirana toward a door. You crack it open and reveal your childhood bedroom. Bewildered, Mirana looks at you. Then, recognition of the significance dawns in her eyes. You glare at her with satisfaction.

Your mother is younger, and you and Mirana are mere children. You're back to the day you and Mirana squabbled

Continue on page 190.

You throw back your head and let out an ear-shattering evil laugh: "Mwah-ha-ha-ha-*ack*!"

Gack! You get a mouthful of pepper.

"*Ah-choo! Ah-choo! Ah-choo!*" You inhaled so much pepper that you're going to sneeze and sneeze and sneeze until the very

END.

AH-CHOO! TO STOP SNEEZING YOU'LL HAVE
TO GO BACK TO PAGE 2 AND START OVER!

over who was hogging the tarts. You were both ordered out of the kitchen because of your arguing.

But then the last of the tarts disappeared. And you discovered tart crusts in your room under your bed. But *you* hadn't eaten the tarts. And *you* most certainly hadn't put the crusts under your bed. The only possible explanation was that the goody-goody *Mirana* stole them. She ate them without sharing even the littlest bite and then shoved the crusts under *your* bed.

The little stinker! She framed you!

Now your mother is questioning your younger selves. "Why are these tart crusts under your bed?" she asks the little you.

Your younger self points at little Mirana. "She put them there!"

"Did you, Mirana?" your mother asks.

You turn to your grown-up sister. "Did you, Mirana?" you say to her, imitating your mother's voice.

"You did!" your younger self insists. "Tell her!"

"Tell the truth, Mirana," your mother says to the young version of your sister. "Did you eat the tarts and put the crusts there, under Iracebeth's bed?"

You may be all grown up now, and this scene may have taken place years ago, but you still roil with hurt and outrage at what you know is about to come next.

Grown-up queen Mirana stands silently, watching the scene from your past sadly.

Suddenly, there's a loud smash! You and Mirana turn to see Alice, the Hatter, and Time crash-land in the corridor. They're in that bizarre contraption Time flew into your private chambers, where you had barricaded your prisoners. Once again, it breaks apart.

Good. You're glad they're here. Now they'll see the truth. Finally! You force Mirana to face her young self.

"Did you eat the tarts?" your mother asks again.

"No," little Mirana says in a tiny voice.

A tiny voice, but a great big lie.

"I'm so sorry," grown-up Mirana says. "If I had just told the truth, none of this would have ever happened. I ate the tarts. And I lied about it."

You hear a gasp behind you as the others realize what this means. At last! Mirana's betrayal has been revealed to all the world!

"I wish I could take it back and do it all over again," Mirana says, her voice choked with emotion. "I'm so, so sorry. For everything."

A single giant tear begins to form in your eye. You quickly wipe it away. "That's all I ever wanted to hear. Really, it was . . ."

Just then, a door opens and a little girl shrieks. Suddenly, you feel as if you can't move. The world changes around you, as if you're looking through rust-covered glasses.

The next thing you know, you're back in Time's castle. Did you faint? You see Mirana's concerned face hovering over you. She helps you up.

The last thing you remember before everything went rusty is Mirana's deeply heartfelt apology.

"Can you ever forgive me, Racie?" Mirana asks softly, putting a hand gently on your arm.

A very unfamiliar feeling creeps over you. Generosity? Kindness? Forgiveness? Happiness? All of the above? You're not sure. It's been such a long time since you felt any of those emotions, you don't know that you can identify them correctly.

"I can," you say, surprising yourself. "I can!

You pardon everyone you ever sentenced to a beheading, and the Hatter promises to make you the perfect hat to complement your, er, generously sized head.

THE END

YOU HAVE YOUR SISTER BACK AND, MORE
IMPORTANT, THE PROMISE OF LOVELY
NEW HATS. NOW IT'S TIME TO GO BACK
TO PAGE 2 AND BE SOMEONE ELSE.

TO PAGE 2 AND BE SOMEONE ELSE.

The White Queen

YOU TUCK your doll under your arm and head off to your daily lessons: reeling and writhing and the various branches of arithmetic—ambition, distraction, uglification, and derision.

Your big sister, Iracebeth, is already at her desk. She's wearing red—her favorite color. Your favorite color is white, so that's what you and your doll are wearing.

She smiles broadly when she sees you, and holds up her own doll, which is wearing a red gingham dress just like hers.

You slip into the seat beside her.

"I have the best idea for a game," she tells you, her eyes twinkling.

You clap gleefully. Your sister always makes up the best

games! She can be awfully bossy, but you still always have fun together. "What's the game?"

"Backward hopscotch!" she tells you.

"Can't wait," you say. Then you quickly fold your hands together on top of your desk as your teacher lumbers in.

"Just think," you say as you and Iracebeth leave the classroom. "Today was a nine-hour day of lessons. Tomorrow we'll have lessons for eight hours, then the next day seven—"

"Of course," Iracebeth says, interrupting you. "We have fewer hours of lessons each day. That, dear sister, is why they're called *lessens*."

Iracebeth knows everything, you think, gazing at

your sister with admiration. "Do you ever wonder why our tutor is a giant turtle?"

"Tortoise," Iracebeth says, correcting you. "It makes all the sense in the world. After all, it is the *Tortoise* who *taught us.*"

Why didn't I think of that? you muse. *She will make such a good queen when we're grown up.*

After a rousing game of backward hopscotch, you find your mother, Queen Elsmere, busy preparing dinner. In honor of the invention of backward hopscotch, you're having dessert first.

"My favorite!" you squeal as your mother places a platter of purplemelon fruit tarts on the table between you and Iracebeth. "Yum, yum, *yum!*"

You love these tarts so much you bounce on your chair, knocking your doll to the floor. When you've settled her back on your lap, your eyes widen. Half the tarts are gone! Tears spring into your eyes as Iracebeth grabs a tart in each hand and shoves them quickly into her mouth.

"You're eating all the tarts!" you complain. You yank the platter toward you. Iracebeth yanks it back. "You can have the crusts!"

"No fair!" you wail.

"No fair!" Iracebeth mimics you and stuffs another tart into her mouth.

The queen turns from the stove and shakes a buttered finger at you. "If you can't get along, there will be no more tarts for either of you," she scolds. "Now out of my kitchen!"

"But—" you protest.

"Scat!" your mother orders.

You and Iracebeth trudge out of the kitchen. You didn't even get to have a single tart.

"Do you want to play with my ant farm?" Iracebeth asks, heading to the staircase.

"Uh, no, I think I'll go pick some flowers," you say. You hope she doesn't decide to join you. She shrugs and climbs the stairs.

You sneak back into the kitchen. You know your mother would give you a tart if she knew that Iracebeth had hogged the platter. But you don't want to get Iracebeth in trouble. She's already been scolded for not sharing.

Your mother is noisily washing dishes with her back to you. Now's your chance. You snatch the last tarts from the platter, leaving behind only scattered crumbs.

You scurry to your room. It's empty. Iracabeth must be getting supplies for her ant farm. You sit at your shared desk, pushing aside the farm and the tiny flea circus. You gobble down the last tart, your eyes closing with the deliciousness. You savor every scrumptious bite.

Uh-oh. Footsteps! You leap up from the desk in a panic. Did your mother see you take the tarts? You swallow the evidence and lick your lips to get rid of every crumb. Then you notice the crusts on the floor. You must have dropped them.

Oh, no! The footsteps are almost at the door! There's no

time to do anything but sweep them under the nearest bed—Iracebeth's bed.

The door opens and you spin around. Little Iracebeth comes in with a jar of ants. She stops and cocks her head, studying you. 'What are you doing?" she asks.

"N-nothing," you stammer.

She shrugs, opens the top of her ant farm, and drops in the ants. "Here you are!" she coos. "A nice new home! I hope we'll be friends!"

Your eyes land on a crust you didn't notice before. You race out of the room.

Uh-oh. Your mother is striding down the corridor toward you with a very serious frown on her face. "Mirana," she says, "come with me."

You slump back into your room, where Iracebeth stands, staring at the crust.

Your mother steps inside and crosses her arms. "What did I tell you? No more tarts!"

"I didn't eat any tarts!" Iracebeth declares.

Your mother's eyes roam the room. Her forehead wrinkles and she crosses to Iracebeth's bed. Oh, no. She's going to find out! You squirm.

Your mother kneels down a moment, then stands back up. "Why're these crusts under your bed?" she asks Iracebeth.

Iracebeth turns and looks at you with hurt eyes. She knows you betrayed her. She waits for you to explain. You shrink far into the corner. When you don't respond, Iracebeth whirls around to face your mother. She points at you. "She put them there!"

Your stomach twists. You are in so much trouble!

"Did you, Mirana?" Queen Elsmere asks you.

Your heart pounds and your tongue feels like it's swollen.

Your sister stamps her foot. "You did! Tell her!"

"Tell the truth, Mirana," your mother says. "Did you eat the tarts and put the crusts under Iracebeth's bed?"

They both look at you, waiting.

Your lips tremble. What do you do? Do you tell the truth? Or do you lie?

IF YOU DECIDE TO TELL THE TRUTH,
GO TO PAGE 203 AND FLIP THE BOOK.

IF YOU DECIDE TO LIE,
GO TO PAGE 204.

YOU KNOW it's wrong to lie. You have only one option: tell the truth. You stand on the bed and take a deep breath.

"My sister's name is Iracebeth!" you state confidently.

Hmmm. This is true but not actually the truth you planned on saying. You try again.

"All the king's horses and all the king's men, couldn't put Humpty together again."

Also true. Odd . . .

You continue to spout facts about Underland and its inhabitants until everyone grows bored and wanders off, unable to remember what the question was in the first place. Including you.

Continue on page 205.

"N0. I didn't take the t-t-tarts." You drop your head. You can't look at your mother or your sister.

"But you did! You're lying!" Iracebeth shouts.

"The crusts are under your bed!" your mother tells Iracebeth. "Don't blame your sister. She's innocent."

You feel even worse. Your stomach contracts. You didn't know lying would make you feel so ill.

"No!" Iracebeth screams. "It's not fair!"

Your mother takes Iracebeth by the arm. Your sister pulls away angrily and runs out.

"Oh, dear." Your mother sighs.

You want to take back the lie, but your mother has gone looking for Iracebeth.

How can you make this right?

You run outside, hoping to find Iracebeth to apologize. You dash through the snowy night toward the town square. You swipe at tears streaming down your face. Poor Iracebeth. How could you betray her this way? You have to find her; you

Continue on page 206.

Well, at least you told the truth—even if it wasn't exactly the truth you had in mind.

~᷄᷅~

THE END

HMMM, MAYBE YOU SHOULD HAVE JUST
LISTENED TO YOUR MOTHER IN THE FIRST
PLACE. . . . GO BACK TO PAGE 2 AND START OVER.

have to say you're sorry, tell her she can have all your dessert from now till eternity. Anything, if only she'll forgive you.

"Oh, no!" you gasp. You skid to a stop at the edge of the town square and watch helplessly as Iracebeth slips, falls, and hits her head. She sits up, holding her head as folks nearby rush to her aid. You wince, seeing her head swell. This is all your fault. She never would have run into the night if you hadn't lied!

You watch sadly as your father picks up your weeping sister. He carries her away with your mother holding her hand. A large tear rolls down your cheek. You wish you could take it all back.

From that day, your sister is different. And as you grow older, her head grows bigger.

You don't think telling the truth now will make any difference. After all, it won't unswell her head. And you don't want to bring up anything that will remind her of that awful evening. Now what you have to do is try to keep her as happy as possible to make up for what you did. But she sure does make that difficult. She grows meaner and meaner as the days go by.

But maybe there *is* something you can do. Maybe you can go back to the past, before all this heartache began. Or go to the future to see if there's something you can do there—er, then.

TO GO TO THE PAST,
TURN TO PAGE 211 AND FLIP THE BOOK.

GO TO THE FUTURE BY
TURNING TO PAGE 208.

IT IS the day your sister will officially be given the crown by your father. To everyone's dismay, and Iracebeth's extreme embarrassment, the tiara Zanik Hightopp tries to place on her head is too small. When he tries to force it to fit, it breaks.

You wilt inside, thinking about how upset she must be. Your own face flushes with embarrassment as the crowd chuckles. You wish they wouldn't snicker. But now they're laughing even louder. Your stomach twists in sympathy. But the way she treats everyone makes her a target. You wish she'd listen to you. You've tried to make her see that if she were nicer to them, they'd be nicer to her.

The crowd's chortles and guffaws incense her. "Off with their heads!" she cries.

Your father thumps the arms of his throne as he stands. "Enough, Iracebeth," he exclaims. To your horror, he declares *you* the successor instead of Iracebeth.

She grows enraged, and her head grows even larger. You hear her threatening the Hightopps. You try to calm her down, but she turns on you, declaring everything to be your fault.

That stops you. Could she be right?

DO YOU GO TO YOUR FATHER AND EXPLAIN
THAT THE CROWN SHOULD REALLY GO TO
IRACEBETH—AND MAYBE EVEN CONFESS YOU'RE
THE REASON HER HEAD IS SO . . . UNGAINLY? GO
TO PAGE 213 AND FLIP THE BOOK.

OR DO YOU GO TO THE HIGHTOPPS
AND TRY TO MAKE AMENDS FOR YOUR
SISTER'S BEHAVIOR? GO TO PAGE 214.

YOU LIE in your crib, playing with your toes. You peer through the bars and see your sister, Iracebeth. She's chewing on a teething ring.

Maybe going back in time wasn't such a good idea. There's not much you can do as a baby.

You do wish someone would do something about your sister's stinky diaper!

THE END

GROW OLDER AND WISER BY TURNING
TO PAGE 2 AND STARTING OVER.

At least the enemy hasn't found me, you think, always wanting to put a good spin on things.

But it's hard to stay optimistic as the sun goes down, the air turns cold, and you realize that you were in such a hurry you didn't pack lunch. Or even snacks. Or purplemelon fruit tarts. Mmmmmm . . .

You can't pretend anymore. You're thoroughly lost. Even the horse wears a quizzical expression.

Oh, dear.

You eventually find your way home. The Lion and the Unicorn agreed to settle their differences over a nice cup of tea; the crown is on your father's head, where it belongs; and you are eating a bowl of soup by a cozy fire.

Continue on page 215.

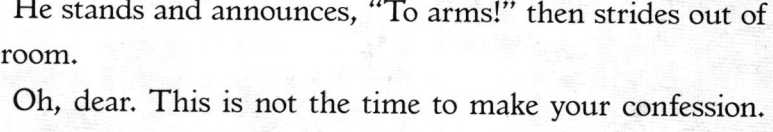

YOU FIND your father in a tower room, where he is reading a large book. You hate to disturb him, but if you don't say something now, you never will.

"Father," you say, "there's something I have to—"

A courtier bursts in. "Your Majesty! They're at it again! The Lion and the Unicorn are battling for the crown!"

Your father slams his book shut. "I have told them over and over: their battle will not be tolerated! They have no right to fight over the crown. The crown is mine!"

He stands and announces, "To arms!" then strides out of the room.

Oh, dear. This is not the time to make your confession. You should help your father!

You quickly don armor and grab a sword, then run to the stables. You're not used to getting a horse ready on your own, so it takes you a while to get saddled. By the time your feet slip into the stirrups, the army has gotten far ahead of you.

Still, you press on.

The horse gallops through meadows, across fields, and then into a forest. Still no sign of the army—or any fighting at all, for that matter.

YOU LAY a hand gently on Zanik Hightopp's arm, hoping to make up for Iracebeth's rude behavior. "I'm sorry, Mr. Hightopp," you say. "My sister wasn't always like this. But . . . something happened when we were small."

"It's fine, Your Majesty, really," Mr. Hightopp says.

You know your sister can be, well, impossible. But if people only understood the reason . . . You've always felt guilty about her *bad* fortune and your *good* fortune. And now . . . now it has cost her the queendom.

"You see," you continue, "it happened many years ago. It was snowing that night. She ran out because . . ." You stop, unable to say the words. You just can't tell him that she ran out because of you. Not here. Not now. "Well, anyway, she slipped in the snow and hit her head. In the town square. Right at the stroke of six. I'll never forget it. . . ."

"I'm sure it has been difficult for her," Mrs. Hightopp says sympathetically.

"The tiaras are beautiful," you add. You glance at the younger Hightopp, still holding hatboxes. He was one of the

Continue on page 216.

Something nags at you, though. You were going to do something before war was declared. You just can't remember what it was. You shrug. Oh, well. Whatever it was couldn't have been that important. It probably all worked out just fine in

THE END.

EVERYTHING SEEMS TO BE QUITE SETTLED
HERE NOW THAT THE WAR IS OVER. GO BACK
TO PAGE 2 AND START A NEW JOURNEY.

first to laugh, you remember. You don't blame him; it was kind of funny. You just hope Mr. Hightopp won't be too hard on his son.

You're called away, still feeling unsettled about the turn of events.

~~~

"Happy Horunvendush Fair Day!" you say to the tall gentleman manning the This 'n' That stall. He's so thin and pale he resembles the shiny white ribbons you're buying from him.

"And to you, Your Majesty," he says, handing you the bag.

"Fine choice, excellent choice," someone beside you says. You glance up and see a familiar face, though you can't quite place it.

The man tips his extravagant hat. "Tarrant Hightopp," he says.

"Of course!" This is the young fellow who assisted his father with the ill-fitting tiara on Toomalie Day.

You glance around for Iracebeth. You don't blame him for laughing on that day, but Iracebeth has held a grudge against him and his family ever since. Luckily, she's nowhere in sight. You sigh. She wouldn't attend the fair, you realize. She can't bear to be around happy people having fun. It makes you sad.

"Fine quality, those ribbons," Tarrant tells you. Then he addresses the vendor. "I'll have one half inch of every color."

You stroll among the colorful stalls, the laughing crowds, and the delicious scents of open-air cooking. You stop to listen to the traveling troubadours and laugh at the antics of the acting troupe. You join in a rousing dance on the grass. It's a day that practically sparkles with happiness.

Then you hear a terrifying sound. "What's that shriek?" you gasp, stumbling into a stall selling chimes and mobiles.

"I'd know that howl anywhere," the vendor says, fear making his voice shake. "It's the Jabberwocky!"

As he says the word, you see the flames. The crowds scatter, screaming. Stalls are set on fire, and trees are blackened. The air is thick with heat and smoke.

You race to where you tethered your white horse. You climb into the saddle, feeling it trembling beneath you. A nearby blast of the Jabberwocky's fiery breath makes your normally docile horse whinny, rear up, then dash crazily around the grounds. You lose your grip on the reins and cling to the horse's mane.

You pat its neck, desperately trying to calm it, but it just gallops quicker. Coughing, you try to somehow get it to turn around and go away from the fair. The panicking, stampeding crowd only adds to its fear, and it skitters this way and that, getting closer and closer to the flames.

Out of the smoke a top hat appears. It's Tarrant Hightopp. He grabs the reins and leads your skittish horse to safety on top of a low hill.

He hands you the reins. "How can I ever—" you begin.

But he cuts you off. "Sorry! I have to search for my family. They're here somewhere."

You grip the reins with shaking hands and he sprints off. You call after him, but he does not turn back. You watch him head back into the smoke, calling for his family.

Tarrant Hightopp lost his family that day, so you were determined to become—along with his friends—another kind of family for him. You long for family, too, as after your parents passed, your sister wrested away your crown, and you are forced to fight her.

It was never about the queendom to you. It's just that she is so frightfully cruel to the Underlandians. You can't stand by and allow it. The Hatter helps you and brings the wonderfully talented Alice Kingsleigh to Underland to defeat the Jabberwocky. You are so sad when you have to banish Iracebeth to the Outlands, but you really have no choice. And it makes you even more grateful to the Hatter and your other friends for the comfort and fun they provide.

But now the Hatter has changed. He has lost his muchness. You decide you must do something about it. He saved you all those years ago; it is time to return the favor.

But how?

SHOULD YOU CALL FOR HIS OLD FRIEND ALICE
KINGSLEIGH? PERHAPS SHE CAN DO SOMETHING.

TURN TO PAGE 222.

OR DO YOU STAGE AN INTERVENTION?

TURN TO PAGE 221 AND FLIP THE BOOK.

The Hatter frowns. "Being late all the time shows either a lack of organization or a lack of respect."

McTwisp's mouth opens, then shuts again.

The Hatter turns to the Tweedle twins. "I've always wondered: which of you is the original and which is the copy?"

"Why, I'm the original!" Tweedledee and Tweedledum say simultaneously. They start bickering, then grow silent.

This isn't how this is supposed to go at all!

"Tell me, Chess," the Hatter says to the barely materialized Cheshire Cat. "Do you disappear because you fear being seen for who you really are?"

Amazing. You've never seen Chess fade grin-first. He must be quite upset.

"Now then, Tarrant . . ." Bayard, the bloodhound, begins.

"Bayard, old friend," the Hatter says. "You have a true talent with that nose of yours. But you're squandering it wasting your time here."

Bayard turns around in three circles, then lies down, resting his nose on his paw.

You need to get this intervention back on track. "We're not here to talk about us," you insist. "We're here to talk about you."

The Hatter sits back at his desk. "Your Majesty, surely you have more vital affairs to attend to. Don't you think this is a bit frivolous?"

Chastened, you gaze at your feet.

"Now please," the Hatter says, standing again, "I have

Continue on page 223.

YOU AND your friends gather at the Hatter's house to stage an intervention. "We are all here because we care about you," you tell him. Reluctantly, he lets you inside.

"We're quite concerned," you begin, not exactly sure how an intervention is supposed to go. "You've become terribly . . ." You search for the proper word.

"Serious?" the Hatter says.

"Exactly!" Thackery Earwicket, the March Hare, bounds over to him and knocks the hat off his head. He grabs a few more hats and starts juggling. "So serious you wouldn't want me to do this!"

The Hatter retrieves the hats and sets them back on their stands. "Is that any way for a full-grown hare to behave? You're not a little bunny anymore."

"I, er, um . . ." Thackery's ears flop down and he slumps into a corner.

The White Rabbit, McTwisp, rushes in the door. "Oh, my ears and whiskers, I'm so sorry to be late."

EVER THE brave and helpful friend, Alice arrives and agrees to go back in time to help the Hatter. Soon she returns to tell Hatter that it is true: his family really is alive! You are so thrilled for him! And for them! And you are extremely happy that you thought to bring Alice back to Underland.

The Hatter is determined to rescue his family. This means you and his other friends must go to Iracebeth's stronghold in the Outlands and confront her.

Oh, Iracebeth, you think sadly as you ride through the woods on your white horse. *Must we always be at odds? Must our relationship consist solely of one battle after another?* You wish with all your heart that things could be different. After all, there once was a time when you actually got along! When you were friends, even.

The Bandersnatch has stopped at the top of a hill, so you tug on the reins. You dismount, then help Mctwisp down from the horse. The poor thing is shaking. That's not surprising; he doesn't usually travel on horseback or at such speed. Mallymkun, the Dormouse, drops from Bayard's back at your

Continue on page 225.

work to do. There are some who take responsibility seriously."

You all file out silently, heads bowed. Well, that didn't go as planned. In fact, from now on, you are all as serious as the Hatter!

THE END

THIS IS FAR TOO SOMBER. TO RETURN TO
YOUR DELIGHTFUL FRIVOLITY AND TRY
ANOTHER PATH, GO BACK TO PAGE 2.

feet. Soon the horse-drawn cart carrying the March Hare and the twin Tweedles pulls up alongside the Bandersnatch, upon whom Alice and the Hatter still sit.

After a quick discussion, it is determined you will leave your mounts here, and then you separate at the castle, the better to search more efficiently.

"This way," Tweedledum suggests, pointing at a corridor to the left.

"That way," Tweedledee says, pointing in the opposite direction.

You chew your lip. This is a horrid place. It's filled with rotting vegetation, roots and vines cling to everything, and your white gown is instantly mud-and-moss-spattered. But you must find the Hatter's family, even if that means getting downright dirty.

"There are so many scents," Bayard complains, sniffing and snuffling with his large nose.

Alice and the Hatter have gone upstairs, so it makes the most sense for you to spread out down on this lower level. "Let's go in pairs. You two, take that corridor," you tell the Tweedles, pointing to the hallway straight ahead. "Bayard, you follow your nose wherever it leads. Mally, go with him. You and I," you say to Thackery, "will investigate—"

"You will investigate nothing!" someone interrupts.

You let out a little yelp as you are all surrounded by Iracebeth's creepy vegetable footmen.

"You are now prisoners of the Red Queen!" the onion-headed footman next to you announces.

Oh, dear. This wasn't part of the plan.

∽∾⟩⟨∽∾

You force yourself to be brave as you stand accused, a prisoner in your sister's kangaroo court. It's all so crazy you're surprised there aren't actual kangaroos bouncing around.

"What are the charges against me?" you ask after she has already announced not only the verdict but the sentence as well.

Iracebeth looks outraged. "You have lied. You have stolen. You are *not* the rightful queen of Underland!"

McTwisp jumps up. "Objection! Where's your proof?"

"I don't need proof!" Iracebeth declares. "I've got better!" She holds up the Chronosphere. "I shall have a confession!" She smirks at you.

You feel faint. Is she really going to use the Chronosphere to go back in time to that terrible day you have regretted all your life? Is that what this is all about?

She throws the Chronosphere to the ground. It pops to full size, glowing, ready for travel. She grabs your arm and yanks you inside.

You're about to find out.

∽∾⟩⟨∽∾

The days roll out under you. You travel farther and farther back in your past, until you reach a time when you were little girls.

Your heart sinks. You know exactly where you are and why you're here. She's bringing you back to relive that moment when you did the worst thing you've ever done in your whole life—the moment you lied to your mother and betrayed Iracebeth at the same time—when you set the events in motion that brought you where you and your sister are today: she filled with irrational rage, and you never able to make up for the accident you caused.

You can't bear the idea of having to watch that dreadful scene again. You've tried so hard to forget it, though it's always nagged at you from that day forward, like a tiny ache that doesn't ever quite go away. Tears cloud your vision as Iracebeth drags you to your childhood bedroom.

"Iracebeth, wait!" you blurt, inches from the door. "I . . . I lied!"

She seems surprised by your confession.

"I ate the tarts, and I lied about it," you continue. "If I had just told the truth, none of this would have ever happened. I'm so sorry."

You look up and meet your sister's eye.

"Forgive me," you plead. "Please. If you can . . ."

Iracebeth's face softens. A tear trickles down her cheek. Your sister looks even more surprised as she says, "That's all I ever wanted to hear. Really, it was."

You embrace her, laughing and crying at the same time. You feel a weight lifted off your shoulders. You should have confessed ages ago. You and Racie have so much lost time to make up for. Then the door to your childhood bedroom opens. Little Iracebeth sees grown-up Iracebeth and shrieks.

And the two Iracebeths immediately turn into rust-covered statues.

Uh-oh.

Rust sweeps through everything! "Come on!" you hear Alice call. You have no idea when she arrived, but you're awfully glad she did.

Weeping, you carry Iracebeth into the Chronosphere. Time sits slumped beside her, weak and sickly. The Hatter looks grim.

You clutch your rusted sister as Alice desperately races across the Ocean of Time before the rust overtakes you—and the whole world. She has to get the Chronosphere back where it belongs.

You bite your lip, watching the terrifying rust wave flooding everything in its path, swallowing people, creatures, all that you love. Then you remind yourself that this is Alice. She defeated the Jabberwocky! She can do not only the impossible, but the *un*possible, too!

And she does! She gets that Chronosphere into place just in the nick of time—and saves Time himself.

As the rust slowly dissipates, your sister's frozen form

starts to thaw. She looks at you and blinks in surprise. You reach your hand out and touch her arm.

You have a question to ask that is long overdue. You gaze at her, tears welling in your eyes. "Can you ever forgive me, Racie?"

Iracebeth stares at you. She narrows her eyes. For a terrible moment, you're afraid she will say no. But then something miraculous happens.

"I can," she says matter-of-factly. She laughs, seeming to have surprised herself once more. "I can!" she cries emphatically.

The two of you embrace again, overjoyed.

You are so happy that you declare it a new national holiday. So it all worked out all right in

THE END.

AT LAST YOU AND RACIE ARE ABLE TO BE HAPPY
AGAIN. NOW YOU CAN TURN BACK TO PAGE 2
AND TRY YOUR LUCK AS SOMEONE ELSE!

"YOU CANNOT CHANGE THE PAST.

IT ALWAYS WAS.

IT ALWAYS WILL BE.

ALTHOUGH I DARESAY, YOU MIGHT

LEARN SOMETHING FROM IT."